A Bathory Uni

Bite OF THE Fallen
SPECIAL EDITION

Get bitten!

BORN VAMPIRE SERIES BOOK FOUR

ELIZABETH DUNLAP

OTHER BOOKS BY ELIZABETH DUNLAP

A Grumpy Fairy Tale Series

The Grumpy Fairy (1)

The Dragon Park (2)

Ecrivain Academy Series

Ecrivain (1)

Neck-Romancer Series

Neck-Romancer (1)

Neck-Rological (2)

Highborn Asylum Series

Freak: A Highborn Asylum Prequel

Stand-Alones

LAP Dogs (coming soon)

This is a work of fiction. Names, characters, places, and incidents either are the product of the author's imagination or are used fictitiously, and any resemblance to any persons, living or dead, business establishments, events, or locales is entirely coincidental.

BITE OF THE FALLEN SPECIAL EDITION

Copyright © 2020 by Elizabeth Dunlap

Cover Art by Pixie Covers; Edited by Pixie Covers

Map designed with www.Inkarnate.com

First Printing: September, 2018

Printed in the United States of America

First Edition: September, 2018

Tales of the Favored: Arthur's Tale and Bite of the Fallen were previously published separately.

❀ Created with Vellum

Dedicated to Jessica Saunders
My first super fan <3

INTRODUCTION

Dear readers,

As mentioned in the description, this is a slow build reverse harem paranormal romance. You may not see the harem for several books, but don't fret! It's definitely there!

If slow build isn't your thing, that's completely fine! But if you don't mind waiting a little for it, keep reading!

Sincerely,

Elizabeth Dunlap

FOREWORD

This SPECIAL EDITION of Bite of the Fallen also includes
the short story,
"Tales of the Favored: Arthur's Tale."

ARTHUR'S TALE

PART ONE

—YEAR: 2043—

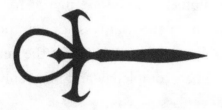

*P*ounding house music blared around me, but I hardly noticed it from my booth in the back of the club. A waitress approached, bringing me the glass of vodka I'd ordered, trying desperately to catch my attention as she leaned in to hand it to me. I barely noticed the low neckline of her shirt, my eyes instantly going back to the target of my stake out, a vampire named Ruben.

"Do you need anything else?" the waitress asked me, only straightening enough where she wasn't leaning over me. My eyes quickly flicked back to her and while I appreciated the way her black halter top curved against her body, I had zero interest in her.

"I'm fine," I assured her over the music as I took a sip of my vodka and checked on Ruben again, still sitting surrounded by women and laughing with his stupid face.

Taking the hint, the waitress folded her drink tray against her body to hide it from my view. "You married?" she asked, searching my left hand for a ring as I brought my glass to my lips.

"Something like that," I told her, and watched her leave only for a second before turning back to my target. I took the briefest of moments to berate myself for having absolutely no reaction to the waitress, or any potential mate, male or female. In my efforts to forget the person who had stolen my soul, I had completely and miserably failed. And I was miserable, I can assure you.

Ruben laughed to the girls around him, holding one close for a rather inappropriate embrace considering the public setting we were in, even with the dimmed lights. All of those girls were gorgeous beyond belief. They should've done something to me, anything. I felt nothing.

My phone rang in my pocket and I pulled it out, watching carefully at Ruben's table to make sure he didn't move before I answered it.

"Hello?"

"It's Olivier." My ex's voice carried her usual deadpan tone. Hearing it sent a wave of panic through my body, because she rarely contacted me.

I pretended to be annoyed, sipping more of my vodka and wishing it would actually give me a buzz. "I'm on a job, what do you need?"

"You have to come back," she said, her tone changing with an urgency I didn't like.

My back went rigid as Ruben got up from his booth, two of the women on his arms. "Olivier, I'm in the middle of a six month investigation into the vampire drug ring. I'm not leaving for some petty committee reason. I've been gone for almost ten years, they can live without me."

Her brief hesitation made everything in the room fade away, including the receding Ruben. "She needs you."

With a loud grumble, I got up from my booth and tried to wade through the throng of humans so I wouldn't lose sight of my target. "Don't spin me that heroic relationship bull, Olivier. She's got Knight, she's fine without me. She belongs with him."

Her annoyed tongue click deafened me. "You are the *dumbest* person I've ever met, and I've met some pretty *dumb* people in my day, Arthur. Did you honestly think that leaving her for ten years would change either of your feelings?"

Yes. That's exactly what I'd hoped.

She heard my silent response and sighed loudly enough to wake the dead. "Of course you did, you dumb ass. Well guess what, it didn't effing work. Stop messing around trying to find Alistair, or the drug ring, or whatever you're *pretending* to do, and get the *eff* back here."

Just exiting the club, I watched Ruben's town car drive away and I swore as loudly as I could, making the humans around me run away in fear. "That's just perfect. You distracted me, and he got away. I hope you're happy, Olivier."

"I'm not, actually. *That's why I called you, you twit.*"

My boots clomped a war path down the city sidewalk, glistening from a recent thunderstorm. "Look, Olivier. I'm not sure what's happened that makes you think you can talk to me like this—" She interrupted me with a string of very insulting swear words and the phone rustled like she had thrown it onto the carpet. I waited patiently for her to pick it back up and continued once I heard her breathing. "I'm still your superior, Olivier, and you're being insubordinate."

While waiting for her response, my heart and feet stopped short, and I almost tripped on the edge of the sidewalk. It wasn't Olivier's breathing I was hearing. It was Lisbeth's. I hadn't heard her voice, or any sound she made, for almost ten years, but I knew immediately that she was the one holding the phone.

A very rare emotion filled me from the top of my head to the bottom of my toes: hesitation. *What was I supposed to say to her?* Hi, how have you been for ten years? Had that second kid yet? How's Knight, is he still treating you right, or do I need to come back and kill him for you?

Have you missed me as much as I missed you?

During my inner turmoil, Lisbeth's steady breaths turned ragged, and I knew she was crying silently. Shutting my eyes to hold everything in, I leaned against a nearby building and smushed my face into the bricks as she sniffed as quietly as possible. Decades of training, steeling my emotions, holding myself so tightly wound nothing got through to me, and just her timid snuffles had me completely undone, without her even saying a single word.

The phone changed hands a third time, and another voice came on, one I hadn't realized I'd missed until he started speaking.

"Did you get all that, icy breath?" Knight asked in his rarely used serious voice. "Stop jerking off and come back." Lisbeth's reproaching words came through too muffled to make out, but I understood very clearly that she was not happy with them asking me to come home, and that solidified her need for me. If she didn't need me at all, she'd be fine with me being there, but the fact that she wanted me meant she would let me be apart from her for as long as I needed.

I could live a thousand years and never deserve her.

2

PART TWO

I *hurried through the building, floor by floor, looking for her. She was my responsibility and I'd let her get away. If she was too low on blood, there was no telling what she'd do.*

When I heard screams of terror, I knew I'd found the right floor. Humans were out in the hall in their dressing gowns, wondering what was causing the bloodcurdling shouts, and calling one of the servants to go find the constable. I pushed past them until I reached a hotel room with the door wide open.

She stood inside the room, dressed in her white nightgown, dots of blood speckled across the back of it. Three corpses were at her feet, and other humans cowered in the corner, hoping they wouldn't be next.

"Adriann," I said as I approached her, my heart shattering into a thousand pieces at the sight of my mate surrounded by her kills.

She turned to me, blood all over her face and chest, the hungry red glow in her eyes receding to their normal green shade. "Arthur," she called to me, her voice shaking as she realized what she'd done. "I'm sorry, I..." Her hand went to her mouth, holding in her gasp of horror, and the other clasped her rounding belly where our baby grew. The humans were getting up, seeing Adriann was under control for the moment. "I just got so thirsty. The baby was so thirsty."

She'd assured me she was getting enough blood, but I should've known she would hide it from me so I wouldn't worry, and now this had happened. No amount of finger pointing could erase this, no matter whose fault it was.

"Arthur!" The rest of the vampire Hunters crowded in the hallway, Olivier at the head, dressed in her proper Victorian get-up with her long black braids in a bun underneath her bowler hat. She looked from me to Adriann, and down at the dead humans on the rug. While the other Hunters entered the room and tried to get the humans under control, Olivier's dark eyes locked with mine, and I knew what she was thinking without asking.

Adriann had broken vampire law, and it was my job to deliver her punishment.

Death.

Olivier walked past me, taking Adriann's bloodied arm, and I left a few Hunters behind to deal with the aftermath and ensure the humans forgot this ever happened. We followed behind the two women until we reached our hotel room on the top floor of the establishment. Olivier settled Adriann into a parlor chair, holding her down firmly by her slender shoulders.

"Adriann has committed the crime of attacking and killing humans, showing no respect for human life," Olivier said in a loud, clear tone, looking up at me as she finished. Adriann had begun to cry, but I stayed where I was, unable to comfort her like I wanted to. She should be in my arms where I could keep her safe and loved. "Arthur." Blinking, I focused on the dark warrior. "I say this as your friend. We're all loyal to you. If you want to take Adriann away to be safe, no one would ever tell. We'd keep this a secret for you. As far as the Council is concerned, she died tonight for her crimes, and that's all they need to know."

I believed in the Hunters and what they stood for, and hearing that my soldiers were more loyal to me than the vampire Council shifted something inside me. I didn't want loyalty to a person amongst my ranks. We had to be loyal to the law, we had to follow the law so strictly that nothing else mattered, because if we let feelings get in the way of our job, then that meant we would let lawbreakers go free. What starts as one broken law could quickly become two. Three. Four. Where would it end?

"We serve a purpose, Olivier," I said once I'd gathered my thoughts. "We are loyal to the Council, not to each other. If any of your mates committed a crime, I would execute them on the spot, and I expect all of you to be willing to do the same." Olivier's mouth curled into a stern frown, her very subtle way of telling me she had several things she wanted to berate me about but would reserve her thoughts until we were alone. Her absolute disregard for my authority was one of the things I liked about her, because if she wasn't willing to question my choices, she couldn't hold the rank of my second in command.

She took a step back from Adriann and crossed her arms over her chest. "Well then, sir. Do your duty."

Stepping across the carpet, I faced the woman I loved, watching tears fall from her cheeks. Could I really do this? Could I end her life? I'd never see her again. I'd never wake up in the middle of the night and hold her tightly against the curve of my body. I'd lose the only person who ever loved me no matter what.

With those thoughts running through my head, I pulled away when she tried to grab my hand.

"Arthur, please," she pleaded, sniffling. "I won't do it again, I swear. You can let me go, they won't tell anyone."

"That's true," I admitted, and her face filled with hope before I pulled out my pistol from its sheath on my belt with a shaking hand I tried hard to suppress.

I'd joined the Hunters to protect my people, and they'd turned me into a monster. They'd turned me into a man who betrays his mate, betrays his love.

"I'm sorry this happened, Adriann, I really am. Please know that I love you, truly, and I wish there could be another way, but it's my duty to uphold our laws, and not even I am exempt from them."

The coldness in my own voice made bile rise in my throat, and I felt all the warmth inside me fading away like a receding tide.

When I held the pistol to her forehead, her green eyes looked up at me with the one emotion I never wanted the woman I love to show.

She was afraid.

Afraid of me.

3

PART THREE

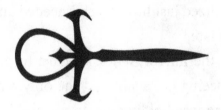

J woke with a start, sweaty and tangled in my
sheets, my chest heaving with ragged breaths
from my nightmares. Centuries had passed and I still
couldn't erase the look on Adriann's face as I held my gun to
her face. Getting up, I walked on unsteady legs to the bathroom sink where I poured some water into my cupped
hands that I splashed on my face.

My reflection in the mirror showed the scarred, tattooed
warrior that had killed his pregnant mate and their unborn
child. I traced the long scar on my cheek with a fingertip, ran
my fingers over the scars on all of my knuckles. It's no
wonder I killed someone I loved, there was nothing about
me that spoke of a gentle man capable of compassion, and a
man like that didn't deserve to be with a woman like Lisbeth.

It had been nearly twenty-five years since I first kissed

Lisbeth. I'd lost count of how many times I'd replayed that memory over and over, despite my failed attempt to forget her. Maybe I'd been wrong to turn her away. Maybe Knight and I could've come to an understanding and shared her. I had a sinking feeling that it didn't matter now with so much time having passed. I'd messed up my second chance at love and I hadn't realized just how much I needed and wanted her until it was too late.

Looking in the mirror, it wasn't hard to picture what it would be like seeing her again, but the only reaction I could see myself doing was holding her to me and kissing her lips long and slow before I told her how much I loved her and would always love her.

I had more scars now, and another tattoo symbolizing what it felt like to leave her behind. All of my tattoos were reminders of my failures, except for the sword rune over my heart that all the Hunters had. The tattoo I'd gotten for Adriann and our baby was on my back so I wouldn't have to look at it every day, but I still knew it was there.

Unable to keep staring at myself, I went back to bed and slept until morning, waking with a buzz from my phone on the nightstand. My eyes still shut, I reached for it and peeked one eye open to check the screen, seeing a text from Olivier.

Tick tock.

I texted back, angry I had to open both of my eyes before I was awake enough to not wince at the sunlight pouring in through the hotel window. *I never said I was coming.*

Her reply popped up within seconds. *Dumbest. Man. Ever.*

Swearing under my breath, I got up and took a very long shower, knowing where I was headed after it was over. I dried off, packed my one duffel bag, and went out to my truck, tossing my bag into the passenger seat before starting the engine and pulling out of the hotel parking lot. The village was a few hours away by car, and I couldn't help but feel more than a twinge of irritation that this little excursion had cost me my investigation into the drug ring.

Someone's head was going to roll.

4

PART FOUR

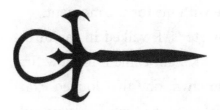

The sun was low in the sky when I arrived at the little vampire Lycan village we'd built around the ruins of the castle. They'd built more houses since I'd been gone, and everyone was gathering for a cookout in the large clearing at the center of town. I pulled into a spot on the street and got out, my eyes automatically trying to see where Lisbeth was. A few of the townsfolk noticed me, saying hello when they recognized who I was, and I caught sight of Olivier setting out paper plates at a picnic table. Her mate, Renard, was beside her, and he noticed me first, elbowing her until she looked up.

Her eyebrows knit together in a scowl when she saw me. "It's about time. Do you always take forever when Lisbeth is involved?"

Ignoring the jibe, I set my bag down on the picnic table

bench. "I'm still unsure why I'm needed here. Is someone sick? Dying?"

"Only your chances of living longer," Olivier responded, holding up one of the plastic knives she was sorting out into cups. I almost rolled my eyes at her, but I held it in. "He's over there." Olivier gestured with the knife and went back to her work, done with me for the moment.

Taking slow steps, I walked in the direction Olivier had pointed out, and Knight came into view first, chasing a little boy around the lawn, one that looked exactly like him and couldn't have been more than five years old. She'd had the second child from her dream. Didn't that mean she didn't need me? She had her beautiful family, and I didn't fit into that.

Kitty was next, sitting in her black hoodie and scowling at the world, but she still managed to smile at the baby when Knight caught him, swooping the child up in his strong arms and tossing him up to catch him again. Balthazar was there, flipping burgers onto the grill, but clearly complaining about it because he hated menial tasks.

Lisbeth wasn't there.

Kitty noticed me first, her back straightening and her hand reaching out to tug on Balthazar's jacket. The Incubus turned, saw me, and shouted to Knight, who turned with the boy in his arms to face me. It was good to see the werewolf, but the look he gave wasn't excited about seeing me. He was relieved. I ignored the way my pulse sped up as Knight approached me, settling the boy on his hip.

"Arthur, this is my son, Jason," he said with his gaze on the child. *His* son. A territory display? Was he already threatened by me? I would never do anything he didn't approve of, surely he knew that.

Jason had Lisbeth's eyes, even if they were dark brown like his father's. He smiled at me with his mother's smile, warming me up right to my center, but I kept my face straight. Knight set his son down and Jason scurried off to tug on Kitty's hoodie strings. When I looked back at the werewolf, he was holding out a hand to me that I shook gratefully.

"It's good to see you, Arthur. We've missed you." Had he? "Some more than others," he added with significance, noting me still looking around for his mate. "I'll take you to her." Kitty and her Incubus father watched us leave, Balthazar giving me a deep, knowing nod. He looked as concerned as Knight did, but then again he'd always loved Lisbeth, and had known her longer than all of us.

Knight led me to the meeting hall, the large Committee room completely empty, but a scent down in the office wing stopped me short. He waited for me to follow him, standing in the doorway to the offices.

"What..." I started, stopping, feeling like a fool, but I had to be straight with someone, it might as well be the one man who loved Lisbeth as much as I did. "What do I say to her?"

Knight's eyebrows rose, his mouth twitching with the effort to not smirk at me. "You're asking me for advice? It seems this is indeed a cold day in hell, amirite?" When I didn't respond, his almost smile fell and he grew serious. "Just hug her. She doesn't need words, she's had words. She needs you. You were there when she fell apart after she thought she lost me, and you brought her out of it. Now she's falling apart without you, and I can't put her back together no matter what I do." A small sigh escaped his lips and he brushed his long black hair out of his face. Some part of me wanted to hug him first, but I ignored it and came closer to the doorway. We stared at each other, appraising the other carefully.

"I entrusted her to you," I told him. "That meant I believed you would take care of her and keep her safe from everything, including herself."

Knight straightened to his full height, several inches above mine, forcing me to tilt my chin up to look at him. Such an Alpha male, this one. Always trying to prove himself to me. If he wanted me to kiss him, he could just ask. "Oh, we're just going to call each other out, then? It's my turn. You promised to stay by her side, and you left her. She's lost so much, given up everything for us, and the one thing she asked you to do was stay by her side. I don't care what your reasons were, you betrayed her. She's never forgotten that, so get in there and do your damn job."

I stormed past him, down the hallway, and threw the office door open to reveal... a mess. A complete and utter pack rat hoarder mess. There were stacks upon stacks of paper on almost every inch of the carpet, dozens of bins filled with snack wrappers, ten empty gas station Styrofoam cups lined up in a row on the desk, and Lisbeth was hidden behind it, humming a tune to herself. She was clearly very distracted, having not noticed my scent as I entered the room, Knight not far behind me, and we occupied the very small patch of floor that wasn't littered with crap.

Meeting Knight's eyes, he was full of worry for her, but he snapped his fingers at me and pointed to the desk for me to get moving.

"Is that you, dearest?"

My entire body tightened upon hearing her voice after so long, my rigid steps taking me around the desk to see her drawing on a piece of paper, charcoal smudges dotted across her face, surrounded by piles of crumpled rejected drawings. The tip of her pink tongue darted out as she erased a few pencil marks and bent over the paper to re-draw the line she was making. Though I only wanted to say three words, the words I'd said to her every night in my dreams, I said the first thing that came to my head.

"The hell are you doing?"

She looked up at me then, her bright purple eyes turning from blank despair to glowing warmth to glistening tears. Her mouth opened and closed as she tried to decide what to say to me, and clearly it was a retort because her eyes narrowed. "I'm clearly drawing a picture, *duh*. Don't you have eyes?"

"Lis, don't you want to come to the cookout?" Knight tried as he leaned over the desk to see her. His tactic was always being nice to her, but sometimes she needed tough love. I suppose that's why I was there, why she needed me.

"She's not going to the cookout, she's putting her stupid drawings down, and she's cleaning all of this up. You weren't there before, Knight, but she pulled this shit when she was under house arrest, and I'm not putting up with it a second time." She stood in a huff and threw her notepad at me, expertly tossing at just the right moment where it would've hit me square in the face if I didn't put my hand out to catch it, which I did. Raising an eyebrow at her growing frown, I looked down at the drawing and saw a girl. Not just a girl, really, because I highly doubted Lisbeth would've gone insane trying to draw a random person. There was something about her that seemed so familiar, but I knew I'd never seen her likeness before, in person or otherwise. She had delicate, thin hair that looked like it had a slight hint of waves, but there was something in her eyes I couldn't look away from.

Knight had apparently seen the girl in Lisbeth's drawings, because he moved closer to me and pointed at it. "Ever seen her before?" I shook my head and he took the notepad, flipping to another girl, sketched out in the same manner, only this one had a mess of curls like Lisbeth did. "What about her?" After I shook my head again, he continued flipping through the pages, filled with drawing after drawing of various things in pencil. Most of them weren't of people, but the two girls appeared quite frequently.

"When did this start?" I asked as I studied each page with

him, unable to stop staring at the first girl when she appeared in the drawings.

Lisbeth answered, sitting up on the desk with a distant look in her eyes I knew well from her time as my prisoner. "Sara's dead."

My lungs released a slow sigh. Lisbeth didn't take death well, not anymore. I took the notepad from Knight and held it up to her, showing a drawing of the first girl. "This isn't Sara."

"I don't know her name, or the other one. But I can't get these images out of my head. Something happened when Sara died, I don't know what. Every waking moment I see them. I can't..." She trailed off, bringing her fists up to beat against her skull, and I dropped the notepad onto the desk in case I needed to stop her from hurting herself. "They won't go away. Make them go away."

Knowing she wasn't having a temper tantrum and there was something seriously wrong with her prompted my feet across the short distance between us until she was in my arms, the one place I'd needed her for so long.

God, I loved her.

My body seemed to sigh with relief, releasing tension I had no idea I'd been carrying for who knows how long as I brushed strands of her hair across her back and her warmth spread over me. I automatically lifted my chin to kiss the top of her head, but I stopped myself at the last moment, glancing back at Knight who was watching our embrace with a calm look as he leaned against the edge of the desk.

Under his placid expression, I tried to pull back to a respectful distance. Lisbeth's arms immediately came around me and she held me so tightly, it brought sharp pains to my chest.

Don't cry. Don't you dare cry where Knight can see it.

I squeezed my eyes shut until my emotions had quelled. I'd let them out later when I was alone, but they had no place right then. I had to be strong for both Lisbeth and Knight. After a few minutes, Lisbeth's arms went limp and she let me take a step back, just enough where I could see her staring up at me but we both still held the other close.

"I can try looking into what's wrong with you, but I'll have to leave–" She grabbed me closer again, not bothering to hear when I continued with, "–for a few days. Christ, woman. Stop packing me to you like a sardine."

"Stop complaining, I'm coming with you," she declared, shoving me away so she could drop down from the desk.

"Samesies," Knight said. "Not getting rid of us that easily."

I crossed my arms over my chest and stared down at Lisbeth's small frame. "You're just going to leave your kids behind? Who's going to watch them, Balthazar? You can't trust him to keep a goldfish alive."

"Kitty is an adult, and Jason can come with us. Meet me at our house in twenty." She picked up the notepad and trotted out of the room so fast I couldn't stop her.

"None of you are allowed where I'm going," I told Knight as I turned to face him. "If you come, your memory of the place will have to be wiped, Jason included. There are no exceptions."

Knight's mouth twisted with a grunt of displeasure. "Lisbeth won't like that. Jason's safety aside, you know how she feels about people messing with her head."

"That's why I'd prefer you keep her here where she and her head are safe." I stayed still, hoping he would do something to help the situation, and he didn't disappoint.

"If you want to make it out of town without her finding out, I suggest you do it right now while she's busy packing. I'll take the heat for it, just go before she notices." When I didn't immediately start moving, he repeated his move of snapping his fingers and pointing where he wanted me to go. "Chop chop, dude. It's your ass on the line, not mine."

I almost, *almost*, reached out to hug him, and I was surprised at how much I wanted to. Lisbeth's mate was just as beautiful as she was, and while I can't honestly say I felt the same way about him as I did for her, I also couldn't honestly say that I never would. Even if I did, though, I'd have to love him from a distance, just as I did her, just as I did everyone.

"*Go!*" he shouted as I stood there staring at him, and I raced out of the room, quelling all of my thoughts so I could focus on getting to my truck in one piece. Hurrying as fast as I could, I got across the lawn where the cookout was still going strong, checking on Kitty and Jason when I passed them, and noted Kitty giving me a reproachful look with her eyebrow raised in a taunt. She knew I would get an earful later from her mom.

"Hope she doesn't kill you," Kitty shouted to me, and she helped Jason wave one of his little hands in farewell, to me escaping or me dying, it was probably both with her sense of humor. Correction, her mother's sense of humor that she inherited. Heaven help what Jason's humor would be with his parents being who they were.

I made it to my truck and put the keys in to start it, pulling out from the spot and starting down the road when I heard the loudest shriek of my life, one that had every bird nearby flying away in terror. Even *my* heart stopped beating for a few moments, and I wasn't scared of anything.

"ARTHUR YOU SON OF A HOE, I'M GOING TO MURDER YOU IN YOUR SLEEP!"

The back of my truck bumped hard like I'd gone over a pot hole, then there was a sweet knock on the truck's back window, and Lisbeth was staring at me from the rearview mirror. She went to the side of the truck and opened the passenger door as we moved down the road, hopping in and closing it behind her. Tossing her bag onto the floor, she adjusted herself in the seat beside me before buckling her seat belt and turning to me with a silent glare that bore a hole into my skull. She sat like that for at least ten minutes, not saying anything, just filling me with the knowledge that she had every intention of punishing me for my misdeeds.

"Stop that," I told her finally, my hands gripping the steering wheel so I wouldn't reach out for her.

"Oh, I'm not stopping anything. You deserve everything coming to you because *you just tried to leave me again, you effing jackass.*"

She had no idea how much she was *asking for it.*

"Can we not do this right now?" I grumped, stealing looks at her in-between watching the road, and she still had the death glare pointed at me. "I'm trying to help you, and you can't come with me, not where I'm going."

She waved her hand, rolling her eyes. "Yes, yes, unless I want my memories wiped, Knight told me. Wipe away. You're not leaving my sight until I say you can. P.S. Thanks for turning him against me, you insensitive prick." My mouth opened to say something along the lines of how I was about to turn the car around and leave her behind, when a laugh bubbled up before I could stop it. I clamped my hand over my mouth, but the damage had already been done, and she let out a burst of laughter that she tried to suppress too. "Why in the hell are you laughing?" she got out between laughs.

My laughter boiled down to a smirk I didn't try to hide as I put both of my hands back on the steering wheel. "It's been a long time since I argued with someone. Since I did anything with someone."

Out of the corner of my eye, I saw her folding her hands firmly in her lap. "Did you talk at least? I know you have a penchant for never speaking when you're alone."

Decades of my life were spent in silence before I met the woman beside me. Silence and crushing loneliness I'd tried hard to suppress. "I did. Silence doesn't suit me much now." It left too much time to think of her, and wish she was beside me. Now that she was, I'd have preferred to never speak as long as I could hear her voice.

Her fingers were turning white from how tight she had them clasped together. Was she trying to resist touching me? "I know the feeling."

As did I.

5

PART FIVE

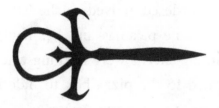

*T*he place we were going to was far enough away that we had to stop for the night and sleep at a motel, one with two beds, I might add. I texted Knight and sent him a picture of the beds when Lisbeth went into the bathroom to take a shower, just in case he thought I would try anything without him to supervise me around his mate.

Don't do anything I wouldn't do, was his response. Helpful. Super helpful.

The shower turned on and I busied myself with taking a pair of sweatpants from my bag that I put on instead of my jeans. I sat down on my bed and closed my eyes, breathing deeply, my ears automatically tuning in to the bathroom, even though I would've never approved of such an invasion of her privacy.

I could hear her even breaths, the sighs that escaped her

lips when she tilted her head back under the water spray. Replaying my memories was nothing like the real thing, being this close to her and hearing every noise she made. She'd crucify me if she knew what I was doing, and I popped back into my own head before she turned the water off and got out of the tub.

The pizza I'd ordered arrived as she left the bathroom, fully dressed in some pajamas and her hair still in damp waves. Damn it, my cheeks were flushing when she met my eyes, and I turned to the pizza box to hide it from her. *I wasn't an effing teenager, get a grip, Arthur!*

Lisbeth took some of the pizza slices and stood next to me as she tilted her head up and dropped the pizza into her mouth, tearing off a large bite with her fangs. She walked to her bed and sat down, shoving more of the food into her mouth. "Forgot how hungry I was since I missed the cookout."

I turned to her, biting into my pizza and trying not to stare too intensely at her mouth. "We'll have to hunt tomorrow morning."

She froze, pizza halfway to her lips, and her eyes flew to me so fast I couldn't tell what she was thinking. "Hunt. Like. Hunting for blood. Hunting humans."

I rolled my shoulders in a shrug. I knew how she felt about it, but I didn't share her views. "As long as we don't kill them, it still fits with the new laws the committee approved."

She finished her food and grabbed a tissue to wipe her mouth with. "Yeah, I'm on the committee, I was there,

Arthur. And I didn't approve of that law being passed. I'm not hunting humans, never again, not ever. I'd rather starve."

Faded flashes of Adriann standing over her kills brought me back a few steps until I bumped against the table I'd put the pizza box on. I shook it off, not displaying a single bit of it on my face.

"Fine, I'll get some bagged blood. We'll drink tofu like peasants."

Rage passed across her face, all warmth gone as she looked at me. "You're such a..." She took a deep breath, holding in the tirade she wanted to unleash on me, tears spilling out from the effort of staying silent, and I almost wished she had because her next words drove a stake through my heart.

"I can't believe I missed you."

6

PART SIX

I hurried through the building again, floor by floor, searching for her. This time was different. It wasn't a memory, things were altered. The humans weren't out in the hall waiting for me to push past them, and a cold sweat went down my back at the knowledge that this wasn't the same dream I'd had for centuries, replaying the night that had changed everything inside me. As before, there was an open door further down the hallway that I moved towards, and when I went inside, my fears were realized.

Lisbeth stood near the doorway, hesitating as Adriann watched her movements, deep in a blood frenzy. I started moving towards Lisbeth, setting off Adriann's rage. She charged so fast she became a blur, intent on drinking Lisbeth dry. Fear was threatening to freeze me in my tracks, but I wouldn't let Lisbeth be harmed.

I ran as fast as I could, just barely making it to Lisbeth's side *before Adriann attacked, and I held Lisbeth close to me, protecting her from anything that tried to hurt her. Adriann swiped at me, knocking me back and away from Lisbeth, before sinking her fangs into Lisbeth's neck. She drained Lisbeth and dropped her body onto the carpet like a discarded food wrapper, then she turned to me, blood all over her face and chest.*

"You can't protect her, Arthur, just like you couldn't protect me," Adriann sneered, licking her bloodied lips.

Gasping in a breath, I came awake in a sweaty heap, searching blindly for Adriann, caught between sleep and awake for a few terrifying moments. Someone warm and soft wrapped me against them.

"Ssh, it's okay, you're okay, Arthur. It was just a dream."

The dream faded, leaving me feeling shattered and weak, emotions I hated. I realized Lisbeth had come from her bed to mine, and she held my head to her chest to soothe me, stroking my short blonde hair with one hand while the other was locked around my neck so I couldn't move away.

"I'm fine," I tried to assure her, but my hands gripped the loose sides of her pajama pants to steady myself. Just a few more moments in her arms. The nightmare was almost worth it for this, but I felt like I was betraying Knight. With that in my head, I pulled away from her and sat back so she was forced to let me go. "I'm fine," I said again, this time making sure she knew I meant it.

Slowly, she reached a hand up and stroked across my cheek, her thumb rubbing my stubble as we stared at each other, and I wanted to kiss her so badly, my heart ached like it was on fire. Far too soon, she dropped her hand and stepped back until she could sit on her bed, still staring into my eyes. "I'm here if you need me." She blinked a few times, looked away, and slid under her covers with her back to me.

Sleeping wasn't going to happen again after that, not even when I shut my eyes and focused on the sounds Lisbeth made in her sleep. I stayed that way until the sun was up and her lips parted with a yawn, only going back into myself so I could watch her stretch under her sheets.

She gave me a sleepy scowl. "Pervert." I smiled where she couldn't see, watching her get up and walk to the sink and mirror that weren't part of the bathroom, taking only a moment to appreciate the way her backside looked in her pajamas. When my eyes went up again, her stare through the mirror was pointed right at me. "That's two inappropriate glances today. Are we going to get to three, because I'm not sure you'll like what I'll do to you if we do."

Oh, I was certain I would.

Without breaking eye contact, she brought her phone out from her pocket and texted someone. Seconds later, my phone went off and I expected a text from her, but it was from Knight.

Pervert.

She giggled at me and went into the bathroom, missing my phone going off again with another text from Knight.

Should we have a talk when you come back?

My chest tightened at the prospect of what he meant, but

my dream had spooked me more than I wanted to admit. I texted him back. *She belongs with you.*

His response had a sigh and an eye roll behind the words. *Whatever, man. Your loss.*

Lisbeth deserved better than me. All I'd ever done was disappoint her, hurt her, and let her down. Knight would never do any of those things to her. And if the day came when I failed her the way I'd failed Adriann... I'd rather die than let that happen.

"You done having a pity party?" Lisbeth asked, suddenly in front of me wearing jeans and a lacy blouse.

I stood, me looking down and her looking up, and I let a whisper of a smirk show on my face. "I don't think you'd talk to me like that if you knew what I think about doing to you every time you mouth off to me."

She wasn't afraid of me, one of the things I loved about her, because not even that phased her as she dared to roll her eyes at me. "You talk big, but it's all talk, and talk bores me. Either punish me or threaten someone else."

A muscle in my jaw ticked as I clenched my teeth as hard as I could so I wouldn't say, or do, the first thing that had popped into my head, because that would've required a very long phone call with Knight that I didn't want to have, and he would probably come and lop my head off after it was over.

"See?" Lisbeth taunted, her mouth curving into a devious smile that made me want to spank the piss out of her. "All talk."

If she only knew exactly what I wanted to do to her right now. If she did, she'd be running in the other direction instead of taunting me on purpose.

I finally turned away and stiffly grabbed my bag, taking it to the bathroom so I could change into a fresh pair of pants and a tank top. I didn't usually wear tanks, but everything else I had was dirty because I hadn't stopped long enough at the village to do laundry. On my own, I wouldn't have cared about wearing a dirty shirt, but I wasn't about to smell like B.O. with Lisbeth nearby.

She was perched on the edge of my bed when I came back out, her bag already packed and slung over one shoulder as she typed away at her phone. Was she tattling to Knight about me? Maybe they were teasing me, or sending gif reactions to mimic my facial expressions. They'd do that and more, make no mistake. They both deserved to be bent over my knee.

"I'm not texting Knight, I'm looking for the nearest diner to have some breakfast," she told me without looking up. "And if you bend Knight over your knee, I'd seriously wonder if you're crushing on him. And in which case, I expect you to ask permission first."

She'd heard my thoughts?

I mean, I knew she had the ability, but she must've gotten more powerful since I'd been away.

"I'm definitely more attuned to people I'm around a lot," she answered to my unspoken thoughts. "But I apologize for that, I was distracted, it slips out sometimes when I'm not paying attention." She got up and slipped her phone into her pocket, meeting my eyes with a slightly timid expression. "Sorry for taunting you. I know it's not really fair."

Shrugging, I gave her a rare smile. "I'd expect nothing less from you. Don't apologize." She smiled back, and I dug my nails into my palm to stop myself from closing the distance between us and kissing her as hard as I could. I waited to see if she'd heard that thought, but she didn't react, just kept smiling and waiting for me to move. "Let's go," I said, somehow feeling slightly disappointed, hiding it as well as I could as I started walking towards the door.

"What's that?" she asked, stopping me with a hand to my left arm, and I almost recoiled away from her in surprise. She pointed to the tattoo I'd gotten in honor of her, reminding me I'd abandoned her when she asked me to stay. It was an infinity knot on my right wrist, and the rope trailed to the inside of my arm, the ends broken off, just like my promise. Staring at it, she came closer, right into the nook of my body, so close her scent was making my head spin, and she flipped my arm over to examine the markings. "You didn't have this one before."

With her so close and distracted, I was free to stare at her face. At the way her long lashes curled up, the way her cheeks curved over her cheekbones, the way her mouth scrunched to the side when she was pondering something. I could easily reach out and touch those things. Easily. She peered up at me then, mid-stare, catching me looking at her with an unfiltered expression, and her cheeks pinkened with embarrassment as she dropped my hand and took a step back.

Great. I'd made her uncomfortable. Let's add that to my list of 'the top twenty reasons why I didn't deserve to be with Lisbeth Bathory.' The opposite list of 'reasons why I should be with Lisbeth' only had one thing on it.

I love her.

That wasn't enough for me. For her.

I cleared my throat and lowered my arm, looking anywhere except where she stood in front of me. "We should head out." She mumbled a response, spinning on her heels and marching out of the hotel room door to my truck outside where she sat in the passenger seat waiting for me to join her. My phone buzzed and I pulled it out to see a text from Knight.

Keep the door open three inches.

How did I ever get roped into dealing with these two on a daily basis?

Oh, right. I loved one, and was maybe crushing on the other.

Dumping my bag into the truck bed, I got into the driver's seat, shutting the door before I started the engine and it roared to life.

"Where are we going exactly?" Lisbeth asked once we'd pulled out of the parking lot and were on the road. I didn't answer, tapping my fingers against the steering wheel as I considered what my answer would be. "I'm assuming my memory of this will be wiped, so you might as well spill everything."

Everything?

She was right, I could theoretically do anything right now and she wouldn't remember. If I didn't have so much damn respect for her, I'd definitely be pulling the car over and start doing something that would earn that phone call from Knight I'd been worried about. But I did respect her, so much it stung me to think of taking advantage of her like that.

"I swear to god, you've gotten so broody," Lisbeth complained after several minutes of silence. "I don't even have to hear your thoughts to know you're having another pity party."

A growl rumbled my chest. "Again, I advise you to stop mouthing off to me." She rolled her eyes, put her feet up on the dash of my truck, folding her arms over her stomach, very deliberately trying to piss me off. "Your memory wipe starts right now. Listen to my thoughts." The spell binding me only stopped me from mentioning them audibly, but my thoughts were safe, and I'd found the perfect loophole. *We're going to see a witch*, I sent to her.

"A..." Her eyebrows raised and her mouth popped open. "A witch? *Witches are real?* How come I didn't know about them?"

I took a few moments to explain how vampires had a non-involvement treaty with the magical world and that those of us who knew about them had a spell put on us so we couldn't talk about them out loud, per the treaty. Her mouth closed when I told her Lycans were part of the magical war between witches and magical beasts, and her natural first question was whether or not Knight knew about them, but I assured her he didn't, because I'd tested him a very long time ago to make sure he never blabbed to her about it as I knew he would.

Lisbeth's face pinched in a frown and she looked away out the truck window. Was she mad at me for keeping secrets from her?

"I'm not mad at you," she told me after a few moments. "I'm just a little disappointed that I won't remember the witches after this. That seems highly unfair."

"I don't make the rules. I wish you could be brought in on the secret, but the treaty is very specific about who can know and who can't. You'd have to be approved by the Magical High Council, and they would still put the binding spell on you." She muttered out a few curse words about what she thought about all of this, and went silent again in contemplative anger. I couldn't deal with silence with her beside me. "Tell me about Jason."

Her arms immediately relaxed and a smile rose on her face. "I had him almost five years ago. It took me nineteen years to get pregnant with Knight." She dipped her chin, trying to hide her widening smile. "When I found out I was having him, I realized I'd given up hope he would ever come. And if he never did, I'd never see the other daughters from my dream." Bending down to her bag, she opened it and pulled out her notepad, flipping to a drawing of the girl that had captivated me. "That's who I've been drawing. They're both my daughters. I'd know their faces anywhere." I slowed down at a stop sign and took a moment to look at the paper as she set it down between us. "She's your daughter, Arthur. I feel it when I look at her. The other one is Knight's, but this one..." Her finger tapped the paper, tracing along the girl's cheek. "She's yours."

The more I looked at the drawing, the more I saw myself in the girl's face, which is why she had drawn my attention like that. I was seeing myself in another person's features. With no siblings, my parents long dead, having a blood relative was as foreign to me as anything I could think of.

"I won't remember telling you this, but I need to say it," she said, making my heart speed up with fear and anticipation. "I honestly don't know how you feel about having a child of your own, but I'm asking you to please ensure I have this girl. I don't know when I'll ask you, but I know that I will someday."

Since I knew she wouldn't remember, I knew exactly how to answer her.

"I've wanted a child of my own for as long as I can remember. When Adriann and the baby..." I stopped, looking away to hold myself together. "I thought I'd never have children again after that. I resigned myself to a loveless, childless life, with no one I could call family."

She picked up the notepad and traced the image again. "Is that still what you want?"

I wanted that girl in my arms, mine and Lisbeth's daughter. I wanted it so badly, my body ached all over. Having her may not have meant her mother was mine, but having a child with Lisbeth was one of the only things I could truly say I wanted.

"No," came my single word answer, because saying more would've revealed how much I'd started trembling all over.

"I won't remember this, so we should probably have a talk about something else. About us." Lisbeth turned to an empty page in the notebook and started drawing with a pencil, erasing and smudging the lead lines as she went.

"I'd rather not," I said firmly, looking over to see her bent over the paper, a look in her eyes I didn't like. "Lis?" For the first time I could remember, I used the nickname Knight used for her, it slipped out with my distracted worry. My hand left the steering wheel to shake at her shoulder, but she refused to move from the notepad.

"I have to..." she said hoarsely, pressing the pencil into the paper so hard her fingers were turning white. "I have to get them back. They're gone, you're all gone. My babies, my mates, I'm all alone. You don't remember me. No one remembers me. Don't leave me, you promised to never leave, not after they took you away from me." Nothing she said made sense. I pulled the truck over to the side of the road and put it in park, unbuckling my seatbelt so I could move closer to her.

"Lis, love, what's wrong?" Speaking to her like that came so easily, like I'd been doing it for years. I pet at her hair and tucked some behind her ears to get it out of her face, looking down at the notebook. She was drawing a woman sitting in the corner, surrounded by darkness, holding an infinity rope exactly like my tattoo. The woman was her, I didn't even have to guess, the way her eyes looked and the wild curls said everything.

"They took you away," she said again, tears streaming from her eyes and splashing onto the drawing. "I can't live without you. I need you." She flipped to an empty page in the notebook so fast she almost tore the paper, and she started drawing a new picture, this one of a necklace with four divided sections, all holding a lock of hair. "You don't remember. You don't love me yet. I just want you to love me again."

Thrusting the notebook away from her, I picked her up and placed her on my lap, holding her so close, feeling her shaking beneath my arms. "It's okay," I soothed, stroking her hair and planting soft kisses on the side of her head. "I'm right here, I'm not leaving you."

Her broken sobs were shattering me from the inside out. "You will. They'll take you from me. I won't see you for so long. I can't bear to be parted from you, but they'll take you away. And..." Her arms reached up to wrap around my neck, pushing us even closer together. "Arthur, it will be a very long time until I accept how I feel about you. I won't remember this, I know I won't. And that means it'll be years until we're together again."

"Lis, stop it." My words were far too weak to be obeyed. "You're with Knight, you should be with him."

"It doesn't matter. I see us together. I don't know when it'll happen, but our daughter will be grown before it does. I can see the future we have together, in both timelines."

"Timelines?"

She whined and gripped me closer. "Just a few more moments before the witches take me. I never told you good-bye. And that I love…" Her words trailed off and she went limp against me. I lifted my head to see her eyes closed. She'd passed out.

7

PART SEVEN

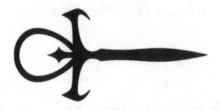

*L*isbeth stayed unconscious all the way to our destination, her head resting on my leg with her body laid out on the front seat, my hand on her neck stroking her skin to reassure myself she was okay. We turned off onto the rural driveway, surrounded by trees and shrubbery that opened up to a clearing where a house stood, smoke coming from the chimney. A few dogs barked at our approach, coming up to the tires as I stopped the truck next to a motorcycle parked outside.

"Chill out," someone barked back to the dogs, and they retreated to the front porch where their mistress stood with a rifle in her hands. The corner of her pierced lips went up at the sight of me. "Well, bust my britches. Arthur Lancaster. Ain't you a sight for sore eyes." I got out of the truck, pulling

Lisbeth and our bags into my arms, and took her to the porch, the dogs sniffing at her shoes.

"Ruby," I greeted with a nod.

"Placid as always," she noted, grinning, and peered at Lisbeth's sleeping face. "Got yourself a pretty girl there, Arthur. Nice job." She tossed her short bob back and reached to scratch at the left side of her head that was shaved to show off her tattoos.

"She's not mine," I told the witch stiffly, but she only grinned wider.

"Then you don't mind if I steal her, do you?" I glared and she laughed at me, lowering the rifle. "Kidding. You should see your face. Come on, we're letting the flies in." She turned and waved me to follow her inside the house, the dogs at our heels, and she closed the door behind us. "Set your girl down there," Ruby said, gesturing to the couch as she put the rifle down on a lamp table by the door. The dogs skirted around me and waited until I'd put Lisbeth on to the plaid couch before sniffing at her and licking her limp hands. "Back up, boys," Ruby ordered, and the two dogs retreated a few feet back, sitting and watching my every move as I put our bags on the floor.

I sat on the coffee table next to the couch, arranging Lisbeth's arms over her stomach and smoothing the hair off her forehead. A fridge door opened and Ruby walked over to me, holding out an open bottle of booze that I took gratefully. She had one of her own that she sipped as she sat on the opposite arm of the couch, staring down at Lisbeth.

"Your girl's aura is out of whack," Ruby observed, swallowing a large mouthful of her drink.

I downed half of mine, not even feeling the bite of the liquor, and set the bottle down on the floor. "That's why we're here, Ruby."

Ruby crossed one leg over the other, balancing effortlessly on the couch arm. "Aww, shucks. And here I thought it's because you liked me."

"Last time I checked, you were a lesbian." I leaned over to Lisbeth's bag and unzipped it, pulling out the notepad.

"Still am," she said, holding her hands out for the pad. "Although I do consider myself 5% bisexual, so if you and cutie here were interested in something later, I'm all for it." Her joking stopped when she started flipping through Lisbeth's drawings. "The hell is this?"

"You tell me," I countered, picking my drink up and downing the rest. "Her friend died and she started drawing like a mad woman. She keeps saying stuff about the future. About... me and her."

Ruby peered over the notebook, eyebrow raised with a taunting grin. "Did she now? Care to elaborate?"

"Not a chance."

She humphed and turned more pages. "This friend, was she human?"

"Your kind." Even though her heartbeat was a permanent sound in my ears, I picked up Lisbeth's wrist to check her pulse, still strong and steady.

"Hmmm, that explains it then." Ruby shut the notepad

and tossed it to the coffee table. "When certain witches die, predominantly divination specialty, their prophecies have to be preserved. Now typically, they go to the nearest witch, but if there's not one for say, fifty miles, they go inside the nearest vessel that has compatible powers. I'm guessing your girl here has had a vision or two of the future?" I nodded and Ruby clicked her tongue, tucking her bob behind her ear. "Yep. That'll do it. What was the friend's name?"

"Sara."

Ruby had just taken a sip of her drink and she spewed it out all over Lisbeth's legs, laughing uncontrollably. "You're shitting me. Sara Campbell?" I shrugged because I had no idea what her last name had been. "Ahh, hell. No wonder your girl is going insane. Sara's powers were wildly uncontrollable." Ruby's smile fell and she looked away. "Sorry to hear she's gone. She was a helluva lady." She raised her bottle in a salute and took another drink. "Rest in peace, baby girl."

I stroked at Lisbeth's wrist, holding her hand tightly. "Is there anything to be done about these prophecies? Can we get them out of Lisbeth's head?"

"Ooo, cutie has a nice name." I glared at Ruby as she got up and went to open a door in the house that led to her bedroom. She emerged again holding a crystal ball in her hands. "We can put them in here, but I'll have to take this to Highborn and show it to the Headmaster. Not that I relish everyone seeing you and cutie doing the do, but it's the rules. Prophecies have to be shared."

"We didn't do anything," I told her, squinting at her

approaching form. She rolled her eyes at me and knelt beside Lisbeth, putting the crystal ball onto her stomach. Before Ruby could start, I reached out to grip her shoulder. "She won't remember the prophecies anymore, right? She won't remember what she saw?" Ruby shook her head and a shank of her hair fell into her eyes. "Don't hurt her."

"Right, like I would even *contemplate* hurting your girl. I know how fast you'd slit my throat if I even joked about that." I leaned back and narrowed my eyes at her. "Okay, I'm going to cast the spell. Hold her down." Ruby moved closer to Lisbeth's middle, and I knelt beside Lisbeth to hold her shoulders down. "Arthur." Her tone brought my eyes over, locking with hers as she peered up at me, the serious look on her face turning my stomach into knots. "Once I cast this spell, I can't stop it until all of the prophecies are in the ball. No matter what happens, I can't stop it. If I do, she'll be lost with the visions, and we won't be able to get her back."

Looking down at Lisbeth, I leaned over her and kissed her forehead, stroking her cheek with my thumb. She'd be okay. I had to believe it. If she was lost, I'd lose my reason to stay alive. I'd be nothing.

"Do it," I said, my lips pressed to Lisbeth's skin for one final kiss before I straightened back up and held her down.

Ruby put her hands to the crystal ball and started speaking the words to the spell, the magic swelling within her in a glowing whirl that burst from her body, blowing everything around the room that wasn't weighted down. The two dogs whined and came closer to lay their heads on

Ruby's leg, lending their support to her magic. Lisbeth's body started shuddering under my hands and Ruby struggled to keep the ball on top of her.

Just hold on. You can do this, Lisbeth.

I hoped she could hear me wherever she was in her vegetative state, hoped that our minds were connected enough where I could reach her no matter what.

Ruby continued to struggle, repeating the spell over and over, almost falling off of Lisbeth a few times. "No!" she shouted. "You're not going to die, hottie. I refuse to let you!" She planted herself on top of Lisbeth's stomach, holding the crystal ball in place no matter how much Lisbeth's body spasmed.

The wind howled, Ruby's body slid around the couch, I threw myself over Lisbeth's head, holding her close to me, and I kissed her beautiful lips.

I love you.

Lisbeth came gasping awake, knocking into my forehead and pushing Ruby onto the floor where the crystal ball rolled away under the coffee table.

"*Piss!*" Ruby shouted, pressing her fingers to her now split lip. "It's not polite to draw blood from the person who just saved you." I helped Lisbeth sit up and she stared around in confusion of her surroundings.

"What just happened? I was... we were in the truck. You told me to stop mouthing off to you, and... then..." She stopped and stared at Ruby on the floor with her dogs beside her. "Who is this? Is she who you were taking me to?"

"I'm just a friend," Ruby explained, bringing her boot up to hide the ball from Lisbeth's view. "Bathroom's over there, you should probably go wash your face, cutie."

"*Cutie?*" Lisbeth asked, her eyebrow raising at the witch. She got up and left us alone in the living room.

I waited for the bathroom door to close before I spoke. "You took her memories of before, when I told her about the witches?"

Ruby got up and took the crystal ball in her hands. "I might've put them inside the ball too. One spell for both, it made it easier." She put the ball up to her face and peered inside it. "Damn. Sara saw a bunch of crazy crap. Not just about you guys either, although I totally see you and cutie making out."

"Skirting the line, Ruby," I warned her as I heaved myself up.

She waved her hand at me. "Yeah, yeah, whatever. Be in denial, I don't give a crap." Lisbeth emerged from the bathroom and Ruby quickly took the crystal ball to a kitchen cabinet where she stored it away from sight.

Looking at Lisbeth, I couldn't help but recall the kiss I'd given her only moments before. She didn't remember it, but I did. I always would.

"Am I cured?" Lisbeth asked Ruby as the witch brought her a bottle of water.

"Yup, you're squared away, cutie." Lisbeth gave me a quick look of disapproval over Ruby's flirting, sipping her water to hide her face from the witch. "If you don't mind, I'd like a word alone with Arthur." Ruby smiled to assure Lisbeth that everything was okay, and Lisbeth gave me one last look before going outside to the front porch. The front door closed and I tossed my head at Ruby to signal we should move further away. Ruby followed me to the back porch so Lisbeth would have a harder time overhearing us.

"I thought you said she was okay now?" I asked, folding my arms over my chest.

Ruby leaned against the wall and mimicked my posture. "She is. This is about something I saw in the ball, and no, it's not you two making kissy face. There's something coming. Sara saw it a long time ago, but she knew there was no way to prevent it. I won't give you all the details because well... not all of it is pleasant, and the wheels are already in motion."

My spine went cold, adrenaline overriding my senses. "What's coming?"

Ruby shrugged and looked down at her shoes. "I wish she knew more specifics, but that's all I can say. Just be ready. Keep that girl and her mate safe. They'll be counting on you. And..." She stopped, pressing her lips together, trying to decide what all to tell me. "In the end, just know she'll find you again. They both will. No matter what happens, you and the werewolf will be by her side. In this time, and... maybe even after that."

There was that mention of time again. What were they talking about?

"Don't dwell on that," Ruby added. "Seeing the future is a

nasty business. Now go home, and if you leave that girl's side again, I'll come kill you myself."

My mouth curled to the side with a dry smile. "I'll keep that in mind."

She saluted me with two fingers to her forehead. "Catch you later, Arthur. My offer with you and your girl still stands."

"Not likely," I tossed to her as I went back inside the house, grabbed our bags, and went to the front porch where I saw Lisbeth already in the truck, waiting with a frown on her face. I joined her, starting the engine and letting it idle as my hands fiddled with the steering wheel.

"I have a feeling I might've said something to you that I can't remember now," Lisbeth said quietly. "I trust that if I asked you to do something for me that you'll do it?"

Our daughter's face settled in my head, proof of the future I was fighting against, the one where Lisbeth would become mine. And gods, I wanted her so badly. I needed her like I needed air. Like I needed blood. If she was right, we had a long road ahead of us, and maybe we had enough time where I'd stop holding myself back from her, where my failures would stop keeping me away, where I could believe that I could keep her safe no matter what.

"You didn't ask me anything," I lied, the words like bitter poison beneath my tongue.

She made a noise and looked away out the window as she had before. "I may not remember saying anything, but I remember planning to. And I've known you long enough to tell when you're lying to me. So do me a favor and at least promise you'll consider doing what I asked."

We left Ruby's house and settled into a silence that bore into me like a drill. As one hour turned into two and we still hadn't spoken, I took my eyes off the road to look at the woman I loved, and I felt myself move one step closer to that future.

I promise.

BITE OF THE FALLEN

1

THE CARNIVAL OF HORRORS

—YEAR: 2053—

"*P*ick a booth. Any booth." My pale skinned mate, Lisbeth, stood next to me with a skeptical look on her face under the blinking carnival lights. The cool spring air smelled like cinnamon, barbeque, and human sweat. It was the perfect combination to make my stomach rumble.

"I don't need a teddy bear," she complained, and wrinkled her nose in the adorable fashion I'd come to love. Standing beside her was our fifteen-year-old son, Jason, who was munching on a funnel cake and enjoying himself much more than his mother was.

"I need a teddy bear," he demanded, mouth full of food. "Win me a teddy bear, dad."

Raising an eyebrow at him, I responded, "What are you, five? Win your own teddy bear." I ruffled his long black curls, a slightly difficult act since he was almost as tall as I was. He stuck his tongue out at me and showed me his half-chewed funnel cake. That's my boy.

Lisbeth furrowed her eyebrows at him this time. "Jason, stop imitating your father." I gasped in mock indignation, but she had me there. Showing my chewed food was one of my quirks. I enjoyed making her squirm, one of the many things we'd started doing to each other after so many years together. Her favorite thing to do to me was eating bacon and not sharing it. Sigh. I loved her so much. She stepped up and gave me a peck on the cheek. "I'm going to the Halloween ghost ride." Unable to help myself, I gently took her chin in my hand and kissed her slowly, enjoying the soft curves of her plush lips.

Daddy like.

When she pulled away, I saw the flush in her cheeks before her smell changed in a way that made my blood heat, and I very much so wished we were alone. I contemplated slipping one of the ride guys fifty bucks so I could get her alone inside one of the fun houses. Time hadn't dulled my attraction to her. On the contrary, I still wanted her as badly as I had the first moment I laid eyes on her.

"No teddy bears," she whispered and licked her moist lips. My voice deserted me with her so close, and I could only nod dumbly. She walked away, giving me the opportunity to watch appreciatively at the sway of her hips.

"Get a room," Jason complained around his bite of funnel cake. "Seriously, you've been bonded for thirty-five years.

Humans hate each other after that long. You two act like you've only been together for two weeks during summer camp." An intriguing scenario. We'd have to act that out later.

Far away from our spot next to the spinning puke-inducing ride, I saw Kitty standing alone at one of the booths. My step-daughter was wearing a black hoodie with the hood over her head. The kids around her were all on their holo-phones, but she paid them no mind and was staring at an aquarium filled with goldfish in the center of the booth.

"I'll be back," I told Jason. He nodded and started walking over to a tornado ride. In the darkness, lit only by the lights on the booths, I walked over to Kitty and stood beside her. The booth was one where you throw golf balls into vases to win goldfish. A few groups of kids threw endless supplies of the balls, trying desperately to get one into the vases, to no avail. The vases had spouts that repelled the balls if you didn't throw them with perfect accuracy. "You not playing?" I asked my step-daughter cautiously.

Kitty might've been thirty-five years old in age, but for a vampire, she was still a teenager. It meant most of the time she was moody and sullen. Standing at the booth, she looked like she was in a bad mood, and she came from a family of volatile women, one of whom was my beloved wife. Lisbeth's temper was terrifyingly hot though, so I didn't complain. In lieu of an answer, Kitty shrugged at me. We got along just fine, but in her mind, I wasn't her dad. It was true, sure, but

I'd been there her entire life. She didn't even give me birthday cards. "If you want to talk..." I offered.

"You're here," she finished, her voice flat and slightly agitated. She sighed, her eyes flicking to the humans still urgently trying to get a ball into the vase and win a goldfish. Her fingers braided and re-braided a few strands of her long black hair that looked exactly like her mother's. "I could easily win every goldfish here without even trying." She could. I could. Anyone in our family could dominate every booth here with little, if any, effort.

"Why don't you? We could get an aquarium. It would look nice in the kitchen." Would that make her happy? I couldn't tell. I'd do anything to make her happy.

"Nah," she answered evenly. "Wouldn't want to steal their hope." She gestured to a new set of ball throwers. "Kind of sucks though. I can never be in the open. I can never show my full power."

I resisted the urge to put my arm around her, just to make her feel better. "You can among your kind, and mine," I comforted.

"It's not the same. You understand." I did. The years before I'd found her mother had been lonely. Living in the human world, and yet never being part of it. We had a nice community now, full of vampires and Lycans, and our two hybrid children. We lived in peace, but we were still hidden from the world.

"Solemn crowd," Lisbeth said from behind me. She kissed the bottom of my ear and hugged me, peeking over my shoulder at the ball tossing. Her purple eyes glanced over at her daughter. "Not playing?" Kitty shrugged again. Lisbeth let me go and hugged her instead. "He'll be back soon, don't worry," she soothed, tucking some of Kitty's long black hair behind her ear. Kitty's solemn mood made sense now. Her biological father, the Incubus Balthazar, went on trips now and then with his life partner, the Succubus Toni. They weren't lovers. I know, that was difficult to believe as their way of greeting each other was a peck on the lips. I long suspected they were lying to us, but since they lived next door, we would've smelled it if they had been intimate.

Kitty was very close to her father. She hated it when he wasn't there. I pulled five dollars out of my pocket and handed it to the booth worker. The human handed me fifteen white balls and wished me good luck.

"What are you doing?" Lisbeth questioned from Kitty's shoulder, grinning widely.

"Shooting deer. What's it look like? I'm winning something for my daughter." Kitty looked away when I said that. *My* daughter. She didn't like me calling her my child, and sometimes I forgot to edit myself. "Sorry," I told Kitty apologetically. Lisbeth's eyes dropped with sadness and she stepped away from Kitty. She too felt upset that Kitty wouldn't accept me, only I wasn't here for emotional crap. I was going to win a fish.

Easily, and with so much skill I felt embarrassed for the humans, I sunk all fifteen of my balls inside the lipped vases designed to make everyone fail. The booth worker's jaw dropped, and she stood frozen for a few moments. One of the other workers quickly stepped in for the sale.

"Nice skills, dude," he said with a smile. "Would you like fifteen goldfish, or you can get three Betta fish, and we also have hermit crabs."

"Crabs," I said with an immature smirk. He got out a little plastic terrarium and picked up three hermit crabs from their tank to put inside it. He handed it to me along with a pamphlet on how to care for them.

"We have some bigger terrariums for them," he began, 'fishing' for more of my money. I pulled out two twenties before he could finish his sales pitch. His smile grew and he grabbed the money, quickly reaching below the booth counter to get a large terrarium with food, a bag of sand, and some decorations for the crabs, along with a water dish.

"Ooo, crabs." Jason came up beside us, his arms overflowing with three Pokémon stuffed animals, and some rock candy hanging out the side of his mouth.

"That better not be our anniversary present," Lisbeth quipped under her breath at the sight of the terrarium. Glaring at her, I held the two containers out to Kitty. She stared at them like I'd just bought her a rifle.

"What..." I jiggled the plastic boxes so she'd take them, and she did after I pushed them against her. "Thanks. I guess."

"*You're welcome,*" I sang and grinned happily. I waited, but she didn't smile at me, and my heart sank just a bit. I ignored it and pulled Lisbeth to me with a tug on her sweater sleeve. "You, Miss Wifey. You get a prize too."

She smiled and placed her slender hands on my large shoulders. "Is it you?"

"Adorable. No. I spotted some lamb tacos over there, and I'm buying you some." She squealed and started dragging me in the direction of the lamb tacos, following her nose until we were standing in front of the food truck and ordering eight of them. Two for each of us. "I could eat everything in that truck," I muttered around a bite of taco. Lisbeth would've retorted, but she was busy stuffing her beautiful, pale face.

I could watch that woman eat tacos all day.

The only sounds around us were that of humans enjoying the fair as we were too busy eating to speak. These kids were *so* mine. I stuffed the last large bite of taco in my mouth and pulled my mate in for another kiss, licking the seams of her lips for a last remnant of the taco sauce.

"Happy anniversary, sexy." She smiled against my mouth, chewed a few more times, and kissed me back. I loved it when she tasted like Mexican food. Lisbeth *con queso*[1].

"Gross," one of the kids muttered. "We're eating here."

Lisbeth narrowed her eyes in their direction. "Didn't I raise you better? There's nothing wrong with your parents kissing."

"Yes, but," Jason defended. He leaned in close like he had a secret and hissed, "You kiss every five minutes. All day long. *It's like a chick flick I can't turn off.*"

Kitty laughed and nodded, licking her pinkie. "Truth."

"One day, son, you'll find a girl. Or a boy. Or... person. And you'll kiss them every five minutes. And when that day comes..." I stepped forward and put a hand on his shoulder. "I will tease you mercilessly because of this moment. Something to look forward to." Pat, pat.

"Son-in-law!!" someone shouted at the entrance of the carnival.

"Oh god, no," I groaned. Lisbeth elbowed me and went to greet her father, Lucas, and Clara, her aunt/step-mother. Once they reached us, Lucas hugged his daughter like they'd been apart for ten years instead of a few hours. He'd missed four hundred odd years of her life, and even though he'd been with us for several decades, there was still lots of time to make up for.

"My Lisbeth," he cooed over her like she was a baby. "Another year with this unruly werewolf. It's not too late for an annulment. I know some people." I tried not to growl at him.

She batted him away and stuck a finger out in admonishment. "That stopped being cute fifteen years ago, dad." She motioned from her eyes to his eyes, signaling she was watching him, and pulled Clara in for a hug.

"Happy anniversary, darling," Clara said happily. "I wish Ana was here." Lisbeth stilled and caught my eyes, then looked away. Anastasia, her mother, was still missing after thirty-five years. We'd all tried to find her, to no avail. My wife and her mother hadn't parted on the best of terms. As

Lisbeth repaired her relationship with her father and aunt/step-mother, she eventually wanted the same with her mother. It had caused many nights of heartache, for all of us. Clara stepped back from Lisbeth and realized she'd brought a frown to everyone's face. "Oh, dear me. I'm sorry. I spoke without thinking."

Lisbeth kissed her aunt/step-mother on the cheek. "We all want her here."

Clara, flushed with embarrassment, turned to me and gave me a hug too. She always smelled like bread. I loved hugging her. "Happy anniversary, Knight. I love you, son." Love this woman. *Love, love, love.* She was the fourth most important woman in my life. Wife, daughter, sister, and then Clara.

When our hug didn't end quickly enough, Lucas huffed and reached in for his bride. "Enough hugs, son-in-law. Don't think I've forgotten about that kiss." He pet at Clara's hair like she was a cat. Yes, I'd kissed Clara once. No, I'm not hot for her, I was simply trying to prove a point to my wife. Clara betrayed me by telling Lucas about it, and he'd never let me forget it since.

"Want one too? Make it even?" I reached out for him and puckered my lips. He gagged in response, because he didn't know how awesome my kisses were.

"Dad, play nice," Lisbeth chided, coming up and embracing me from the side. "We still need to get some stuff for Cameron and Merrick. I'm thinking more Pokémon stuffed animals."

A scream in the crowd drew our attention. It wasn't a, *'whee this ride is awesome!'* scream. Or even a, *'ermahgerd I love carnivals!'* scream. It was of the, *'please help I'm being attacked by a face-hugging alien!'* variety. We sprang into motion towards the noise as more screams filled the air. The sounds led us to the one place in the carnival we hadn't explored yet.

Herman's House of Horrors.

A little tent shanty sat on the edge of the carnival, resembling a sad, little remnant of the circus in Dumbo, like after his mom had wrecked everything and it all went to hell. I was half tempted to sniff test some of the stains on the tent fabric, just to be sure I didn't need to use a blacklight before entering.

Just as we arrived, a group of humans came out, probably the source of the screams. Some of the women were clutching their hands to their breasts in shock, and the men looked equally green. I recalled humans having a similar response when I'd first seen a moving picture. They were silly creatures.

"Smell anything?" Lisbeth asked me in a whisper. I shook my head and took her slender hand in mine. There were too many smells there for me to single anything out. Too many bodies. She wrinkled her nose, under the same predicament.

"Herman," Lucas commented, looking up at the sign. "What kind of mystical name is Herman?"

I snorted out a laugh. "Nice point, dad." Lucas huffed at me calling him dad, which is exactly why I said it.

"Let's go inside," Clara suggested with a smile as if she hadn't seen the terrified humans around us.

The screams had drawn in other humans to see what all the fuss was about, and we all piled into the dilapidated tent. Three rows of low wooden benches sat in front of a stage that had a tall box in the center, covered with a red drape. Jason led us to a bench near the middle and we all sat down.

"I feel like I'm at a cultish religious gathering," Lisbeth complained, crossing her legs. "If they bring out a little boy and say he has healing powers, I'm out." Kitty brought the hermit crabs up to her face to inspect up close. Or maybe she was trying to block out everything as the tent filled up. Once every seat was occupied, a flamboyantly dressed man appeared from behind the stage.

"Welcome all to—" He swished his silky cape around, trying to look mysterious. "—Herman's House of Horrors!" Herman bowed and his hat fell off onto the ground. Everyone snickered, watching him fumble to pick it back up.

"Humph," Lucas said in front of me. "This is where the screams came from? Were they screaming at his bad breath?"

The man onstage hadn't heard the complaint and went back into his dramatic pose. "This is no ordinary house of horrors, I guarantee you. We have something truly..." He paused for effect and smiled to reveal fake vampire fangs. "...terrifying."

A few humans actually had the nerve to gasp, and we all glared in their direction. Fake fangs were scary? Wait until they saw real ones, they'd all piss themselves.

"I need a volunteer from the audience," Herman said, flicking his hand towards us. Lisbeth popped up literally faster than any of the humans could raise their hands, and walked up to the stage without prompting. "Ahh, an eager beaver, I see!" Herman chided in a teasing tone. "What is your name, my dear?"

Lisbeth's purple eyes found me, and I felt a wave of fear from the look on her face. What was she sensing that I wasn't? Hackles raised, I edged forward on my bench, as close as I could get to her without standing up.

"Erzsébet," she answered loudly, enough where everyone in the tent could hear her.

"Ahh, a strange name. Are you foreign?" She nodded, internally rolling her eyes over his small talk. "Well, Erzbet."

"Erzsébet," she corrected with a sniff.

"My apologies. Erzsébet." Herman walked closer to her, intending to put a hand on her arm. My wife didn't allow anyone except family to touch her, but she graciously let the human take her arm and walked a few steps over to the covered box. "What do you think is in this cage here?" She leaned in for a delicate sniff, earning a chuckle from Herman, and immediately recoiled so fast, she practically disappeared. Herman laughed and tried to pull her back to him. "Now, now, my dear. Nothing to be afraid of. There's no way what's under there can harm you."

Our group was on edge now from Lisbeth's behavior. Jason leaned over to me, fear coming off him in waves. "Dad, what's wrong? What's up there?"

Every inch of my skin crawled, and being so far apart from Lisbeth when she could be in danger was pulling against everything inside me.

"Here, let me show you," Herman said, at the same moment when I heard Lisbeth in my head.

'Get Arthur here now. Protect the children.'

I shot up from my seat, Jason yelled for me, and Herman yanked the cover away from the box, effectively destroying with one action any semblance of normalcy we'd had for decades.

What was in the box, you ask?

Standing inside, amidst thick metal bars, restrained with heavy chains on its decaying skin, was a vampire drone.

A drone. In our city.

A white hot pulse of fear went through me, laced with drone related PTSD, stronger than anything I'd felt in the minutes leading up to that moment. We'd fought off drones before, many years ago, and it almost destroyed Lycans and vampires both. I pushed through the anxiety and started moving towards the stage. The humans had screamed that screech again, the *please save me from the killer zombies'* kind, and most had stood up from their seats, blocking my way to Lisbeth.

Like a stupid, naïve human, Herman was chuckling again and waving his hands to calm the crowd down. His laughs weren't kind. They were almost jeering, like he thought our reactions were adorable. "I want to remind everyone that there is nothing to fear."

"Dad, what is that?" Jason said from beside me, grabbing at my arm.

I could feel fear lifting off him and reached a hand back on his shoulder to steady him. "I left my holo-phone at home, text Arthur." He flipped his wrist to bring up his holo-phone and I saw him text Arthur *'SOS at carnival. Weird zombie thing with the humans.'* My wife's right hand would be here faster than Barry Allen if she was in danger.

Lucas held Clara to him, his fragile human bride. "How did he restrain it?"

On the stage, Lisbeth pulled on Herman this time, her face pinched with worry. "You should get out of here. It's not safe."

He waved a hand with a chuckle, ignoring Lisbeth's wise attempts to move him away. "My dear, I know what I'm doing. The creature has been properly restrained."

Human brains were funny. If not presented with proper proof, they easily replaced fact with a truth that was easier to accept. The crowd was doing just that, and calming down enough for us to move to the front of the stage.

Lisbeth met my eyes and shook her head as I tried to climb the stairs to get to her. She'd want me to stay with the children, just in case something went wrong.

"How did you make it?" a woman asked.

"Special effects, right? Boring!" a man countered.

"Controlling it with a remote, I bet," another said.

Herman was offended by the doubt. "This is not a robot. This is a real creature." He stepped closer to the cage, Lisbeth reaching out to stop him as Jason tripped beside me and Kitty knelt to help him up. "He's restrained, he can't hurt anyone. You'll see."

"Jason, you okay?" I asked, and my nostrils flared with the fresh scent of blood. Jason had cut himself on the edge of one of the wooden benches, and I wasn't the only one in the tent smelling the vampiric-like scent his blood had.

Distracted from Jason's injury, Lisbeth didn't have time to stop Herman from unlocking the cage. The drone roared and immediately backhanded Herman away from the stage. He landed with a squishy snap at the edge of the tent. The humans could no longer pretend this wasn't real, and they ran from the tent as fast as they could, not caring who they knocked over or stepped on. In the confusion, the drone leaped from the stage and landed on Jason, fangs out and ready to drink him dry.

Letting out a battle cry at the sight of her baby being threatened, Lisbeth dove, expertly landing on top of the drone. I went for its legs and we wrestled to get it off of Jason. The drone drew his head back, slamming into her nose, cracking bone and making her blood flow. She swore and rolled off the drone to tend to her nose. Lucas swooped in to take her place.

"You okay?" I asked her. She gave me a thumbs up while Kitty and Clara inspected her bleeding nose.

The drone tried to kick me off his legs and unseated me long enough to get the jump on Jason. He sank his fangs into Jason's arm like a tick. Forgetting her injury, Lisbeth roared in a terrifying screech at the sight of her child being bitten, and grabbed the drone by the throat in a death grip.

"You bite my son, I rip you apart," she informed the mindless monster. With her bare hands, she tore the drone's fangs out by the root, and not going to lie, it was a huge turn on. She was so strong and powerful. Nothing stood in her way.

And cue Arthur! He pushed into the tent with one of those neck restraints people use on dogs. Lisbeth lifted the drone up for Arthur to put the loop around the bleeding monstrosity's neck and tighten it.

"Everyone okay?" he asked as he pulled the drone up by the neck. I didn't miss the look he gave Lisbeth where she couldn't see, one of concern for her wellbeing and longing to be near her.

Lisbeth and I zeroed in on Jason's arm and the bruising bite mark on it. He had vampire blood, so he would probably be okay. Probably. If not, I shuddered to think of what Lisbeth would do to whoever created this drone. I doubted Herman was involved with it. My eyes went over to his still form on the ground, and I knew by his scent that he wasn't going to get back up.

"Jason, I'm so sorry," Lisbeth sobbed, bringing him in for a kiss on his curly head. "Does it hurt? Do you feel strange?"

Being a teenage boy, he pushed his mom away and his cheeks flushed with embarrassment. "Mom, stop! I'm fine." He pulled the sleeve of his shirt down over the bite.

"He'll be fine," Arthur assured, because we totally asked

him. Lisbeth scowled in his direction. "I've been bitten by a drone before. Not like it can make you a vampire when you're already a vampire."

"Vaewolf," I reminded Arthur. "He's a vaewolf." He waved a hand at me in dismissal.

Arriving after her commander, Olivier appeared in the tent opening. "I'm here, what's... Oh." She saw the drone struggling to grab onto anything from where it sat on the ground, held by the tool in Arthur's hand. Its mouth dripped blood from Lisbeth taking its teeth. "That. Is gross. Okay, you guys get back to the village. We'll fix the humans. Meet you there in an hour."

2
MUSINGS IN PIG LATIN

*I*t takes a village, as the saying goes. A village to rebuild the two supernatural races we'd all come to love after the turned of mass destruction happened thirty-five years before. Where once stood a castle that vampires hid behind to protect their outdated society, there was now a meeting hall where both vampires and Lycans were equally represented. The members of the new ruling committee were elected, and while their term was literally for life, it was in the rules that they could be unseated if their people thought they were being misrepresented.

The werewolf seat was held by me, after a unanimous vote, and I was doing a fabulous job, if I do say so myself.

"The Itty Bitty City Committee will come to order," I said with a thump of my hand on the wooden half circle desk we sat at.

The Lycan member, Jamie, sunk his face into his hand to rub his temple in irritation at my opening line. "EVERY TIME."

The turned vampire member, Hades, was equally broody, with his Dracula type outfit and a pale, gaunt complexion to match. Fitting, considering his name was Hades. I had a suspicion he'd named himself that, because what self-respecting mother would call her son Hades? "It's been thirty-five years and you refuse to stop using that name. I propose we create another werewolf."

"Denied," Balthazar countered smoothly. He had his feet up on the desk in front of his seat on the committee. He represented the Bicus interests and had arrived back from his trip just in time for the meeting.

"Knight, must you goad everyone?" Clara whispered next to me. She represented the human interests. Having humans represented on the committee brought all kinds of contro-versy since we remained hidden from their world, but Lisbeth was quick to point out that while we were not part of the human world, our world did not exist without them, and therefore their interests should be protected. Humans could be so lucky to be protected by her.

"Let's focus, please." My wife pat my hand from her spot on my other side. "We have a very big issue to discuss." A flick of her fingers and Arthur opened the side door to drag in the vampire drone. Muzzled and trussed up like a Thanksgiving turkey, it still made everyone in the room flinch at the sight of it.

"Were there more?" Hades asked, his eyes betraying his fear, the fear we all felt. He pulled at a strand of his lanky, red hair to quell his emotions.

Lisbeth held out a comforting hand so he wouldn't yank his hair out. "So far, no. It's the only one we've found. Thank god. We have dispatched Olivier and Renard to search for more in the area." She reached for a glass of water with a shaky hand. I put my hand on her knee and rubbed it to calm her.

'It's okay,' I thought, pushing my thoughts through.

I heard a response, her voice echoing in my mind. *'The last time one of them was on these grounds, we almost lost everything.'*

Pretty neat trick, right? Years of focusing on her connection to me meant we could talk telepathically. Go ahead. Be impressed.

It goes without saying that almost everyone had drone-related PTSD. Time could never erase the war. Kitty, sitting on the far end of the table, was one of two who didn't react with utter terror. Kitty had only been a baby when the turned war happened, and while she understood what everyone else was feeling, she couldn't relate the same way. The second of us showing no reaction was Arthur, because duh. Dude was a brick wall. He could be peeing his pants over his worst nightmare and you'd never see it on his face. The only time that icy structure cracked was when he looked at my wife.

"Where'd the thing come from?" Kitty asked. She also had

her feet on the table to match her biological father's pose, and she was making it clear she didn't care about anyone with her hood pulled over her head. *Teenagers.*

"We haven't I.D.'d him yet. Someone had the good sense to burn his fingerprints off," Arthur told her, running a hand through his short, blonde hair, trying to look all cool and handsome. Pssh. "His DNA is useless since he's part vampire, and his face is rotting off so we can't use facial recognition." Arthur was right, this drone was literally decaying in front of us, and it was *gross.*

"I don't remember the other drones decomposing like this one," I noted grimly. Ugh, the smell coming from that thing was enough to turn even my stomach, and I'd eaten my fair share of questionable refrigerator leftovers.

"It could be age," Jamie reasoned. He brushed his long black braid against the table in thought. "Mayhap this is what happens if a drone is allowed to live for a long time. Unless I'm incorrect."

Lisbeth shrugged, tapping her fingertip against her kissable lips. "No idea. I could ask my father. He might know."

Clara drummed her thumb against the table, as agitated as I'd ever seen her. "We still need to find out who created him."

Lisbeth tensed beside me, making me tense in response. "I can read him if no one objects." With extra blood, she'd be able to read the creature's thoughts and see who its master was. No one objected, so she took my offered arm and sunk her fangs into my skin. It was equal parts pain and pleasure.

Not like a drug high, more like a release of pressure with the sting of her teeth. I both liked and hated it. Finished, she stood and planted a kiss to my head on her way around the table to the drone. Arthur held it up for her to put her hands on its sickly face. A wrinkle formed on her forehead and she closed her eyes to focus. Almost instantly, she recoiled and moved away like the monster was a viper about to attack her.

"Alistair," she said under her breath.

Shit.

Chili cheese dog pizza. That was about the only thing that could've taken my mind off our situation, and my wife knew how to play me like a fiddle. She waltzed into our yellow house like a delivery goddess and placed the takeout pizza boxes onto the kitchen island.

Dinner was the one time of the day where we put away our holo-phones, told our lovers to wait until bedtime, and spent time together as a family. Equally important was when once a month our little community had a block party cook-out, and we all spent time with our brothers and sisters. That wasn't happening for a few days, so it was time for pizza.

With a kiss to her cheek, I helped my wife bring plates and drinks to our large dining table as our family trickled in. Jason poked a finger in Kitty's ear and she responded with several well-placed slaps. Cameron kissed Merrick on the forehead, their conversation in Japanese not stopping for one second. Clara delicately placed a napkin on her lap and handed one to Lucas. He stared at it like it was a grenade, but allowed her to lay it over his legs. Balthazar had Toni on his knee, looking like a sexy photo shoot with their effortless perfection as they both sipped drinks in martini glasses and spoke together in a language none of us knew, their special Bicus language. Lisbeth sat down next to me, sliding a hand up my knee, and we all started grabbing slices of pizza.

Several languages spread around the table as each small group traded inside jokes and had private conversations that everyone except me added to. Leaning back in my chair, I took a bite of pizza before putting an arm around my wife.

"Iway ikelay ouryay uttbay[1]," I said to her in a sexy voice. She turned to me with a mouth full of food and her eyebrows knit together in confusion.

"Did you just say something in pig latin?"

"Well, I'm the only one here that doesn't know another language. I have to say sexy things to you somehow."

"Opstay aringstay atway ymay aughter'sday uttbay[2]," Lucas ordered from the other side of the table.

Jason, mid-chew, added, "Ancay eway opstay alkingtay aboutway om'smay uttbay[3]?"

Lisbeth leaned into me with a sarcastic serious face. "Look at what you've done!" she hissed.

"I'm bringing culture to the peasants," I remarked and took a swig of my drink. "Also I like your butt. Sorry not sorry." She rolled her eyes at me, but still came closer for a quick kiss.

Lucas grabbed his goblet from King Arthur's table (still unsure if he was joking about that) and stood up dramatically. "On this blessed day of giving thanks, I am thankful—"

"Dad, it's April."

"—for family. Long may we sit at this table talking about frivolities, while somewhere in the world lurks a danger none of us can foresee."

I stood up too and held out my grape soda. "I'm thankful that I'm not the weirdest person at this table. Love you, dad." He scowled at me, toasted my toast, and sipped from his goblet. Dude didn't really hate me, he just liked disliking me, on principle, since I was boinking his daughter on a regular basis. I bet hating me made him feel like a traditional dad, one who liked to polish his rifle when the boyfriend came over. And don't think he's never done that, because he has. Lucas was like a television, constantly changing stations and mimicking the things he'd seen, or simply getting lost in the past. I'd seen him impersonate Arnold Schwarzenegger more than once. It wasn't that bad either.

Lisbeth tugged on me until I sat back down. "Thank you for the toasts. We're all very thankful for our family. And we'll be more thankful when we're all safe from threats. So here's to those that would stand against us. May they all fall on their faces in front of their crush." She held out her glass and we all brought ours up before taking a sip.

Kitty was the only one sitting there like a turtle, unwilling to move or participate from under her hood. Her only movement was picking up her pizza and putting it back down after she'd taken a bite.

What was wrong with her? Her *real* dad was back, she should be happy. No more spending time with substitute dad. Lisbeth's hand slid over my shoulder and she gave me a quick squeeze. I didn't have to say what I was feeling, and I was tired of being upset over it after all this time. There's only so many times you can come to your partner upset about the same thing, even if she never complained.

Luckily, there was a pound at the door to interrupt my thoughts. Only one person in our community ignored the doorbell and used his fist to announce himself.

Arthur.

Lisbeth wiped her hands against each other to get the crumbs off and stood up, walking over to answer the door. Icy boy was standing there like he'd arrived to take her out for a night on the town. "Evening, Arthur. We were having some pizza. Would you like some?"

He shook his head and bent low to Lisbeth's face for a hushed whisper. The love between them was painfully obvious, it made my heart hurt to see it. I was respectful of what they shared and had no reason to be jealous. I hurt for my wife, loving Arthur so much but he refused to be with her. I watched him carefully, just to make sure his hands stayed where I could see them. I was still a territorial werewolf when it came to my pack, and if he ever got out of his noble BS funk and wanted anything beyond friendship with my wife, I expected him to ask me first, even if it would be an automatic yes on my part.

His icy blue eyes fell on me, something passing between us that I had no name for, and he gave me a deep nod before leaving the way he came. Lisbeth came back to her chair without comment, a fresh flush across her delicate cheeks.

'Was that about the... thing?' I thought to her.

She lifted her leg to lay over the other and pushed against my hip with her toe. *'No. And stop calling it the thing. You know it's important to the three of us.'*

"What'd he want?" Lucas asked, mouth full of pizza.

I saw her consider whether to mention whatever Arthur had said, and I felt a small fear that it had in fact been about *'the thing'* and therefore she was trying to spare my feelings on the subject. Turns out she was just being mindful of the fact that we were all eating.

"The drone destroyed itself by trying to escape the cell Arthur put it in. It was... apparently very messy." Half of the table set their partially eaten pizza slices down at the thought. With a curled lip, Kitty put hers on Jason's plate and he gobbled it up like a puppy, while Balthazar and Toni were unfazed. I suspected they weren't even paying attention, but that wasn't uncommon for them.

The meal effectively ruined, everyone said their goodbyes and went home while the kids went to bed and I stayed behind to help clean up. Lisbeth looked over at me when I stopped in the kitchen doorway. She gathered up a large handful of silverware from the dishwasher and turned away to start putting them in their drawer.

"I'm assuming by your comments that you're not as 'cool' with my plans as you said you were, which would've been nice to hear before we did my treatment last month." Her tone was even, and it took a practiced ear to know she was upset. I could only feel sad because I knew exactly what this meant to her, but somehow, I couldn't be completely on board. And I wanted to be. My brain and my heart were doing a nasty duel inside me. When I didn't answer, she knew I was in turmoil inside and couldn't organize my thoughts into a response. "Look, Knight. I love you. I do. And I want you to be happy."

"And I want you to be happy," I pointed out. My defense was weak, and I knew it. "You're settling for less than what you really want."

She pressed her hands together under her nose, taking in a deep breath to calm herself. "I need to have a vampire child." I sighed and raked a hand through my long hair, looking away. "Knight, please. There are so few Born vampires now, everyone is doing their part to repopulate."

I knew she wasn't doing this for any other reason than helping vampires rebuild their species, even though she'd known this entire time that the third child in her dream was Arthur's. As soon as the Born vampires pointed out she hadn't done her part to help them repopulate, we had to have a conversation with him. It goes without saying he was reluctant to offer his services as a test tube baby daddy, but when it came to Lisbeth, he could hardly say no.

"And you couldn't hold off until... until things changed between you?"

Her eyes darted around the room, a glistening layer of unshed tears forming in her eyes. "I can't wait for that anymore. I saw her in my dreams. I know she's going to happen."

"One vision and you got never-ending baby fever," I joked dryly.

"Can you blame me?" she asked, her mouth pulling into a deeper smile. She looked so happy, it twisted my stomach. "Knowing that the children from my dream will exist? It's why I never gave up hope for Jason, even though it took me nineteen years to have him, and it wasn't like we weren't trying. When I knew he was coming, and when I held him in my arms and saw those eyes looking up at me, it was the most beautiful moment. After this child, our daughter will come, and I don't care how long it takes to have her. Their souls are burned into my heart. I've never seen them again after that night, but I know what I saw. And who knows, that might not have been a final look. We could have more children after the first four. I definitely woke up before the dream was over, I could feel it."

Sighing, I walked over to her and folded her into my embrace. "I know it matters to you. I know. I just wish things could be different."

She traced her fingers over my bicep and my entire body

sighed with relief from her touch. "Arthur is a good man. He understands the situation, and he's prepared to help raise our daughter with us. I think he's a little excited about it." The corners of her mouth slowly fell from a smile to a frown.

The only problem I had with this situation was Lisbeth's unconscious hope that this baby would've been created out of love, that Arthur would stop pushing her away after thirty-five years and just admit he was a lying jerk face when he told her he didn't want her. A blind man could see the truth in his eyes when he looked at her. He was absolutely crazy about her, time hadn't dulled that one iota.

Leaning down, I kissed her forehead so tenderly she gripped my shirt with her fingers. "I'm sorry, Lis. I'm sorry this didn't happen the way you wanted."

She pushed away, sliding some hair behind her ear and turning back to the dishes. "It's fine. I'm not upset." She was such a liar. A beautiful, loving, heart-broken liar.

"Maybe if you did a little dance, twerked until your butt was chafed, he might reconsider?"

She burst out laughing. "You are a bad man." Oh, I definitely was. "Are you sure you're comfortable with this? We can wait for a few months to try again." I shut my eyes, floating my hand through her hair in contemplation.

"If this is what you want, no matter the circumstances, then it's what I want too," I mentioned, kissing her head. She started protesting, so I hushed her with a finger to her lips. "I want you to be happy."

"I am," she said against my finger. I sighed in defeat, she stood up on her tiptoes and pulled me down for a passionate kiss, one that made my blood burn with an unquenchable fire. I picked her up, dishes unfinished and pizza boxes still on the table, and carried her to our bedroom, shutting the door with my foot.

3

ARTHUR IS STUPID

*E*ven with the drone effectively dead, our problems were far from over. Alistair was making a comeback, one that no one wanted, like smallpox, and fashion from the 1990's. Arthur had spent the better part of a decade searching everywhere for the dude and came up with bupkis, so we had to face the reality that whatever move Alistair made, we would be blind until it came to the surface. And that wasn't sitting well with anyone.

We spent an anxious few days debating our next move, and the best distraction was our monthly cook out. Lisbeth and I packed up what we needed and we set up in a corner of the council hall lawn. Arthur approached carrying some of his famous chocolate chip cookies, and Lisbeth squealed when she saw them in his hands. An enigma this guy was, being a hardened warrior, and knowing exactly how to bake the perfect cookie. He stopped right next to where I was grilling some ribs and burgers, closer to me than her.

"All for me!" Lisbeth declared, trying to take the plate from him, but he lifted it up on his fingertips, holding his arms up above his head where she would never reach it. *"Asshole,"* she complained, putting her hands on her hips and pouting at him. If Arthur could ever crack a smile, it was with Lisbeth standing in front of him with her bottom lip sticking out. His mouth was stark straight, but the twinkle in his eyes was unmistakable, and Lisbeth knew she'd won when she saw it. He produced a baggie with several cookies from his back pocket and handed it to her, earning another squeal from her lips.

"Pssh, I spend hours slaving over these ribs and you're excited about cookies," I joked, not serious in the slightest. Lisbeth bit into one of Arthur's cookie with gusto and she started smelling like pure love, most of which was not directed at me for the moment.

"You know how much she likes pastries," Arthur defended, but he gave my meat a sniff and a look of appreciation, just in case I was actually wounded.

"Mk crssn nx tm," Lisbeth said, mouth full to the brim with cookies. Arthur raised an eyebrow at her, and she just smiled back as she chewed. I almost translated her food talk, but Arthur was already rolling his eyes at her.

"I'm not making croissants."

"Scw yu," she protested, and stuck her tongue out at him with cookie all over it.

Glaring, Arthur set the cookies down on the table we'd set up beside the grill. "You're so gross." She flung her leg out to kick at him but he deflected without looking. "Two kids in and you're still as immature as ever."

"Three if this works out," she noted, taking more bites of cookie. "But I don't intend to change. Ever."

"God help us if this baby turns out like you," he said as he took a cookie for himself.

"Hey," I interjected, having enjoyed watching their banter up to that point. I stuck my spatula at him in warning. "You know Lisbeth is awesome, and you'd be lucky for your little spunk baby to turn out like her."

Arthur took one of my sodas and opened the bottle-cap top without a tool, *show off*, took a long sip and leaned against the table next to me as Lisbeth walked away from us to meander through the crowd of our friends.

"How's she been?" he asked quietly, watching her laughing at a friend's joke.

"Why don't you ask her?" I met his eyes to see his typical look of 'you're asking me a dumb question.' "She's fine, as you can see. Sometimes she has her moments, even though you've been back for ten years now. It really did a number on her, you going away like that." He tipped his drink back for a sip, watching me turn some burgers over. "You still love her, I know you do."

"Why do you think I left?"

I met his eyes again and he had his guard down, giving me an unfiltered look of longing. I knew it was for Lisbeth, but the sight of it brought a flush to my cheeks. *What was wrong with me?*

I looked down to get control of myself again and poked at the ribs with my spatula. "How'd that work out for you?"

"It didn't." He took another drink and the look disappeared behind his icy wall until he saw her again, and he looked so... forlorn. It tore at me, but I didn't know why. I had to stop myself from reaching out to take his hand.

"Cheer up, bro. She's got your maybe baby in her now. That's pretty close to everything else." I smiled through his death glare and we watched our girl, both near and far away at the same time.

With the cookout over, the committee gathered the next night to discuss the fate of the drone.

"The thing is dead," Jamie pointed out. He was a clean cut, hair braided into tight braids, family man type of guy. "I don't see the reason to panic further. It's not like there are dozens of them on the streets. It was just one."

Hades crossed himself at the thought of more drones. "You mind yourself, son. You weren't there for the war, you don't understand." Hades had been a rogue vampire at the time and came out of hiding after the war was over. None of us had the heart to point out that he hadn't been there either, because his words were correct.

"We know it came from Alistair, and that's enough to be

concerning," Lisbeth said gently, trying to keep everyone as calm as possible. "Olivier and Renard are still out searching for more drones. Meanwhile, Toni is doing some lab work on the creature, trying to see if we can find out where it came from and how long its been alive."

"And then what? We sit on our hands until Alistair makes his next move? I like that plan less than pretending this isn't serious." Hades sent a pointed glare to Jamie to emphasize his point, and Jamie flipped him off as an answer. Those two. They should just kiss and get it over with.

Toni appeared through the door Arthur was standing at. I caught his eyes on me and we both looked away quickly. Toni's sun-kissed skin and luscious curves fueled her seductive aura, and it had an effect on Jamie and Hades despite their dislike for her, and Hades' asexual orientation. Both pretended to be very interested in something on their nails. The succubus had a folder in her perfectly manicured hands, which she passed to Lisbeth before standing in front of the committee. Lisbeth opened it where Clara and I could see, peeking over her shoulders like good little nosy bodies.

"Preliminary testing suggests," Toni started. Ugh, science jargon. Can't she just say, so I did the thing and this is what I found out? I realized I'd zoned out because she was talking about spore samples or something like the dude was made from mushrooms. "Since the flora testing was negative, I went instead to finding out the age of the drone. He's been that way for ten years."

Lisbeth's forehead wrinkled in thought, and she passed

the folder when Hades wiggled his fingers at her for it. "Why ten years ago? There wasn't a drone issue then."

"My best guess?" Toni offered, shrugging. "An experiment. The drone was imperfect. I conducted multiple tests, this is unlike any drone I've ever seen."

"So Alistair is being all 'Frankenstein-y,'" I surmised, sneering at the thought. "That's great. What if he starts going bigger than just one?"

As soon as I said it, we collectively realized that he probably would. After all, last time he pulled all the stops when he turned an entire city into drones. He clearly had no reservations about mass turnings, and he'd had decades to plan his revenge on us. All because the Born vampires had abandoned him centuries ago.

If only we'd caught him sooner. *Someone* hadn't done his job well enough. A rage built inside me, focused on the blue-eyed soldier standing at his post, whose gaze on me went from an almost smile to deadpan annoyance when he saw the look I was giving him. My fingers thrummed against the desk in front of me and I waited for everyone to stop talking so the meeting would be over. As soon as Lisbeth said meeting adjourned, I was out of my seat and across the room before she'd even gotten up. Arthur's eyes stayed forward even when I stood so close I could smell his cologne. And man, it smelled good. Damn it.

"Her office. Now," I demanded, locking eyes with him. My fists clenched, I made my way to Lisbeth's office with Arthur on my tail. She joined the line behind him almost immediately, yelling something to Kitty to make her stay behind. Once I reached Lisbeth's office, I stopped at her desk, and even the little dancing sunflower on the wooden surface couldn't make me smile.

"What's this about, Knight?" Arthur asked evenly. Lisbeth closed the door and stood in front of it. I could hear every breath she took as if I was right beside her. That helped calm me, just a smidge. I wished, more than ever, that I was a normal Lycan and I could just shift to show everyone how ticked off I was. Instead, I had to actually live with the rage, become one with it. No amount of anger would let me hide behind fur and claws.

"Ten years," I ground out finally, opening and closing my fist. "You had literally ten years to look for Alistair, if that's in fact what you were actually doing. You. The Hunter they all feared, the one who never missed his mark, who never came home empty-handed, was bested by a feeble old man. One that's going to come after us now."

"I see. It's my fault he's still out there, is that it? And yes, by the way, that's exactly what I was doing for most of those ten years." His blasé attitude was enough to enrage me a second time.

"You could've prevented this if you'd done your job and caught him the first time," I accused bitterly. Lisbeth's sudden disapproval of my words was like a smell in the air. I knew exactly what face she was making without turning around.

Arthur let out a very small sigh. Gigantic, for him. "And

you think blaming me for your inadequacies will make it better?"

I turned on him so quickly, Lisbeth jumped forward to make sure I wasn't about to tear his head off. "What the hell does that mean? You want to push me, icy breath?"

A muscle ticked in his jaw, and he watched Lisbeth put her hand on my chest to steady me. "You say I'm to blame because I couldn't find him after a decade? I didn't see you helping. Was that because you didn't have any blood to do your little werewolf tracking parlor trick? Or maybe you didn't realize the ramifications of not finding him until it was staring you in the face?" Even after all that, the only indication of his anger was his hands clenched into fists. We glared at each other for much longer than necessary. Only Lisbeth by my side kept me from lunging at him and taking a chunk of him with me.

"I didn't..." I swore under my breath and looked away. *Damn him.* Sometimes he knew me better than I knew myself. Why did this pissant get under my skin so much? "I didn't volunteer because I knew Lisbeth would come with me."

"I know, and I understood that." His fists relaxed. Back to the normal Arthur. "As if either of us can tell her what to do." We shared a rare smile then, in respect for our lady.

"Standing right here," Lisbeth stated, waving her spare hand.

The tension disappeared and Arthur loosened up just a bit. Lisbeth had that effect on both of us. He really did love her as much as I did. "Knight," he said calmly, his hands almost reaching out before he stopped himself. "I know you well enough to understand that your anger is only because you know your family is in danger. We all are. We did everything we could to prevent this."

Lisbeth searched my eyes with hers, her fingers pressing into my skin. "You know that, right?"

I picked her pale white hand off my chest and kissed every finger gently, only feeling slight shame that Arthur was watching. *Let him watch.* "Yes. I do. And I'm sorry about the tirade. I'm just worried about my..."

"Inadequacies?" Arthur offered, like a cheeky git.

"Yes, thank you, that's perfect." I flipped him off and leaned against Lisbeth's desk. She fit between my legs when I pulled her to me. Right where I liked her. "What are we supposed to do?" I asked absently, my fingers working the fabric on Lisbeth's hips.

"We're supposed to discuss these kinds of things with the committee," Lisbeth chided with a smile, her finger touching right on my stomach where my scars were. I tried not to react with Arthur standing there, and I pulled up off of her desk, taking her hand and kissing her palm.

"Sure, fine. Let's do it." We marched out of the room the way we came and into the meeting room chamber. Everyone was still there chit chatting, thankfully. "I have a proposal for the committee."

Hades curled his lip at me, but he lifted a hand in acknowledgment. "You have the floor."

"We send out as many as we can to find Alistair and stop him before he puts his plans in motion. No matter what he's plotting, we have to stop him. Everyone has to help. Everyone."

"We're a committee, not a parliament," Jamie pointed out cautiously. "We can't force the people to do anything they don't want to do." Or anything *he* didn't want to do.

"Volunteers then," I conceded, though the mere thought of people saying no made me uncomfortable. "As many as we can get."

Balthazar clicked his cane against his foot in thought. "It is bewitchingly easy to believe that Alistair remains on the loose from an oversight on our part. I'm glad my ego is too large for guilt trips. We all did what we could to stop Alistair, and now we're going to do even more. I'll be the first to volunteer."

"Dad," Kitty exclaimed, pulling on his jacket sleeve with worry building on her face. "It's too dangerous."

He reached back to her, pinching her hooded cheek, and they shared a smile that made my stomach hurt. "I'm aware, my crumpet. The risk of further danger outweighs the risk at present."

Kitty stepped forward, chin up and determined. "Then I volunteer as well."

Lisbeth, Arthur, and I chimed out a harsh 'no' before Balthazar waved his cane at us. "While I realize no one is asking me, and I don't get a say in the matter, I believe the girl is old enough. It should be her choice."

Lisbeth bit back several remarks, making her face twitch for a few seconds. "I... you.... This isn't..." Finally, she facepalmed so hard Captain Picard would've been proud. "Let's discuss it later," she murmured and then pointed a finger out to Arthur with her other hand. "Hush, you. I can manage my daughter." It didn't matter how many times she, or I, told him to be quiet, he was never going to.

Arthur stiffened and directed a minuscule glare at her finger. "I was merely concerned for your mental state should she be in danger." Of course he was.

"Anywaaaay," Hades said, drawing it out. "We should hold a city meeting for volunteers."

Jamie was on it, eager to get away from our family drama. "I'll go post it on the website and social media. Hades, want to go door to door?"

"You mean talking to people I don't like?" Hades chewed on it with a frown. "Fine, whatever. Let's go."

As soon as they were gone, Lisbeth's hand dropped and she focused on her daughter's face. "Kitty, I understand you want to go out and save the world."

"You have no idea how *old* you sound saying that," Kitty quipped. All three of us guys took a step back from the women, just to be on the safe side. It would either end with blood and tears or just tears by themselves. Neither option was preferable.

Lisbeth's face appeared blank, but I could see the fire raging underneath as she fumed at her child. "I literally remember exactly what it was like to be your age. *Literally.*

Perfect memory." Kitty attempted and failed to not roll her eyes.

Mayday, mayday. Abort mission. Save the women and children. Tell my mother I loved her.

Lisbeth let out a string of unintelligible words before placing her hands together against her mouth and sighing. "Okay. Let's do it your way. You can go out with whomever you want and look for Alistair."

What.

"I'm sorry, I just died. What did you say, dear?" I asked her sweetly.

"You all heard me, don't be dramatic," Lisbeth sauced, waving her hand in dismissal. "Vampires need to get out and be on their own when they're old enough, and I don't get to decide what that age is. It could be thirty-five, it could be one hundred and five. Either way, you have my permission, but you don't need it. I certainly never did."

Kitty brightened, like her night sky had turned to sunlight. When had I last seen her that happy? "Really? What about you, dad?"

Balthazar shrugged with a smile. "Your mother is correct. It's not our job to stop you from growing. Do whatever you want. Date boys. Date girls. Get a tattoo. Maybe one of those piercings the humans like."

Making a noise of disapproval, Lisbeth held out a hand to stop him. "Okay, whoa there, cowboy. I said she could go hunt for a dangerous criminal, not get inked."

Kitty didn't care, and she vaulted into her mom's arms for

a hug. "I love you, mom." She pulled back and I desperately wanted to offer her a high five or a fist bump. I knew she wouldn't go for it, because she never did. I had about as much of a chance of getting Arthur to high five, and he also refused to do so.

"I assume one of your team will keep you fed?" my wife asked Kitty, petting her daughter's long curls with silent worry. Kitty nodded. She didn't have a companion, so all the vampires close to us rotated who she fed from every day. "Good. Please make sure they are very discrete with their feeding."

Kitty rolled her eyes. "I know, mom."

"Does that mean I can go out too?" Jason asked, popping up at the front door to catch the last of the conversation.

That time, all five of us shouted out a crisp, "NO!"

4

SILVER SPICE

*A*fter nightfall, once the meeting was over and everyone was in bed, I went outside in the cool, spring air to our backyard where Lisbeth was swimming in our large pool. Her lithe body sliced through the water like she was parting the seas. She dipped under and surfaced with a smile in my direction.

"I seem to recall a time when I found you swimming late at night," she said, pushing her wet hair back. Even with the threat of Alistair looming over everything, I was very appreciative of the amount of skin she was showing. Her black two-piece bathing suit was a favorite of mine. It had many straps decorating it, including ones that hugged her cleavage.

"As I recall," I noted huskily. "That was the first time you saw me shirtless. I've held up hope all these years that you liked what you saw."

Lisbeth's hair still managed to curl even when soaking wet and it formed a tussled halo around her as she walked slowly up the pool steps. "I very much so liked what I saw, I can assure you, as much as I pretended not to notice." Her mouth twisted into a seductive grin.

Gulp.

"I very much..." My voice gave out when she stepped up to me and ran a single finger down the middle of my shirt, speeding my heart up so much I was going to need a dunk in that water before too long. "Oh, you are a bad woman. Remember that city meeting they held when we disrupted the entire city's sleep with very loud pool nookie? I'm not saying the words, 'aquatic coitus' in public ever again."

Her bottom lip stuck out and I wanted to catch it with my teeth. "A disappointment, since I rather enjoyed that aquatic coitus. That's why we bought that lake house up in the mountains, where no one is around for miles."

The shiver that ran up my spine was very uncalled for since I was trying very hard to control myself around my insanely hot mate.

"Wife," I admonished with a judgmental finger. "If this wasn't the most inopportune time, we'd be off to that cabin right now."

She looked down and all the heat left her face. "Right. Going away for the weekend isn't going to happen with the hunt for Alistair starting. We got so many volunteers, but we have to stay here to map out where everyone's been, and technical things, and blah blah blah." Sighing, she leaned her head against me, her damp hair making a wet spot on my shirt. "I was a different woman during the war. Stronger, ruthless. I've put her away since then, and I went back to the Lisbeth that loved peace and making jokes. The Lisbeth that spared Simon's life. War Lisbeth might not have made that choice. I don't want to bring her back."

"Hey," I soothed and pulled her face up to stare into my brown eyes. "War Lisbeth was so hot, it was insane. She was terrifying to be around, but she would've spared Simon, I guarantee it. You can be both versions of yourself. I'll be right here for you every step of the way. And like I promised you long ago, if you go too far, I'll be here to stop you. Scouts honor this time." I kissed her forehead gently, and moved slowly down to her lips, capturing them with mine in a dance that heated my blood so intensely, I could swear it was exactly like the first time I'd kissed her. I'd always react like a hot-blooded teenager with her in my arms.

"We're going to have another aquatic coitus issue if you don't move us inside *right now*," Lisbeth whispered when I let her up for air.

No further prompting necessary.

I lifted her up and her legs wrapped around my waist, right on the money, and I let out a whimper because my feet couldn't carry us back inside fast enough. The back door slammed, but we didn't notice, our kisses reaching a fever pitch. I backed Lisbeth up against the kitchen counter and swiped off a few bowls that were in the way so I could lift her on top of the surface. The bowls clanked into the sink and one fell off onto the tile floor, bouncing noisily. The racket we were making didn't disturb the house at all.

This house was soundproofed for a reason.

That was also the reason why no one disturbed us when clothes hit the floor, and things got very *aquatic* indeed. Your kids only need to walk in on that once before they realize it's not safe to be out of bed after nine pm.

Several coituses later, not all of which were against the kitchen counter, I tucked my wife beside me in our large canopy bed. With the curtains closed around us, we were in our own little world. I kissed her sweaty temple and moved her hair from my face before resting my head against the back of hers.

"If Alistair walked in right now, I don't think I would have the strength to get up," she whispered contently, still trying to catch her breath.

Smiling, I kissed her hair, feeling a bit winded myself. "Good, my job is done. Also same. Not even a drone army could move me from spooning you. Mostly because I'm spent." Her hand moved from underneath mine and I saw her reach back for a fist bump.

I loved this woman.

Her fist appropriately bumped, she settled into my spooning with a sigh. "We have to find him."

"Sssh," I hissed, holding her closer. "Our bed is a neutral bubble. We agreed on it. There's even a plaque on the wall. No talking about serious things here. Only coitus and cuddles. We have enough to worry about without making our bed stressful." She made a noise meaning she agreed, but begrudgingly.

We lay together, our bodies entwined, until Lisbeth's breathing deepened and she was asleep. I stayed there with her in my arms and felt that spike of fear creeping back over me. Fear that Alistair would try again to take my family from me, and this time he would succeed. I had much more to lose now. Our children, for starters. Lisbeth's parents, my sister and her mate, Balthazar, and even Arthur.

My arms tightened around Lisbeth, bringing her even closer to me. What if she lost me? What if I was the one who perished in the fight? If she was gone, I wouldn't recover from that. If I was gone, what would happen to her?

She twisted in my arms. I'd woken her up. "What's wrong?" she whispered, turning to look up at me with a sleepy smile, and I kissed her lips gently to reassure her.

"Nothing, love. Go back to sleep."

Working together, the committee took over a week to figure out where each team of volunteers would search and for how long. The main issue was that we didn't have a picture of Alistair. It was difficult to say, 'Go find the thing even though we have no idea what the thing looks like.'

Merrick had seen his face, but she couldn't draw well enough to make a picture, so since one of the Lycans was a Police suspect artist, they worked together to come up with a depiction of our man. Her perfect memory meant accurate attention to details. When it was finished, she brought the drawing to us in the meeting hall where we were all gathered around our long desk sorting papers and putting together agendas.

Lisbeth took the paper from Merrick, and her eyebrows raised, her mouth forming a delicate 'o', her cheeks flushing slightly. I'd only seen her make that face when she saw pictures of Tom Hiddleston. Balthazar and I peeked over her shoulder, eager to see the face of this mystery vampire.

He looked like a damned vampiric old spice commercial.

"Holy hell," Lisbeth whispered, eyes fixed on the drawing. "Silver romance alert. Is this a steamy book cover model? Where's the creepy mastermind?"

"I know," Merrick said with a dreamy grin. "Dude is wasted on being evil." She flicked her fingers to the women in the room. "I can make copies for you guys. Just saying."

Lisbeth whimpered in complaint when I took the paper from her. "Okay, let's stop mooning over the psychopath," I told her. Damn it. He was pretty fine. For a dude. "Focus. He's evil. Let's repeat that to ourselves. He's evil. He's evil."

"Alright, god." Lisbeth took the paper back and handed it to Arthur, who also examined it carefully to see what the fuss was about, and judging by his reaction, he thought Silver Spice was sexy too. I'd been around vampires enough to know they weren't so guarded about liking both men and women. Most of them were bisexual, my wife and Arthur included. Jury was still out on Kitty and Jason. "Tell

Marie to make small copies for everyone, and laminate them as well." Arthur nodded and was off to Marie's office. Lisbeth cleared her throat, brushing her hair off her shoulders to try and remove the image from her head of Silver Spice.

"Man's not even in the room and he's already causing Incubus-like havoc," Balthazar muttered, sliding some papers into envelopes. "Imagine what it'll be like when he's actually in front of us."

Kitty hadn't seen the drawing, but she shuddered from where she sat putting papers into folders. "Imagine him having an aura and we all just stop fighting and beg to be his servants."

My wife's mouth curled up in a frown. "I never beg."

Ha. *Liar.*

"Should there be an instance of a siren's call, I will be there to make you come to your senses," Hades said confidently. "I'm not attracted to either gender."

"I highly doubt it will come to that," Lisbeth told him, hiding a smile. "But in case it does, you're our last line of defense."

Scary thought.

We finished putting everyone's folders together, including airplane tickets and passports, and handed them out once all the volunteers had gathered in the meeting hall. Kitty was going with a small group of Lycans and vampires around her age. They looked like a biker gang, complete with mohawks, leather jackets, and tattoos. Kitty getting inked was definitely a possibility now. Maybe she'd get a unicorn, or something awesome. Just no tribal art, for the love of god.

Maybe I should get a tattoo, and we'd be tattoo twinsies.

Lisbeth saw where I was looking. "You're thinking of getting a tattoo?"

"Mind reader," I muttered.

"I don't need to use my powers to know your thoughts," she retorted with a smile. "Just please, for the love of all that's holy, no Chinese characters. I saw a lady once that thought her arm said 'pleasant blessings,' but it really meant 'lawn chairs.'"

I moved behind her and started braiding some of her curls. It was very good for stress, and she always let me do it. "You don't mind if I get a tattoo?"

She shrugged. "I don't own you. You can do what you want with your body. Plus, I'm surprised you don't have any yet. Every adult Lycan we've ever met has at least three."

I leaned in and planted a slowly heated kiss on her neck. "I've never liked anything enough to put it on my skin before."

She let out a noise that was not appropriate for mixed company. "I know that's not true, considering how many times you've watched Deadpool 5: Deadpoolery."

"Hey," I complained sharply, poking her side. "That movie is a classic. I don't care what that Tomato site says." She giggled at me, and I leaned in for more neck kissing. She'd started making more of those noises, kind of the point, when Arthur approached us, effectively ruining it. Lisbeth straightened with him so close and I went back to braiding her hair.

"We should move outside," Arthur said. His icy blue eyes glanced at my hands and back to her face before she nodded and corralled the troops out the front door. Outside the meeting hall on the front half-circle drive sat several retired school buses painted white that we'd purchased a few years back. Our community liked getting together for camping and cookouts at the nearby lake, and the buses helped us transport everyone.

Lisbeth helped each group onto the buses, and once they were all loaded up, we drove to the airport. I sat next to my wife at the front of the bus that held Kitty, Lucas, and Clara. They too had volunteered to help find Alistair, though I suspected they were also going to try and find Anastasia. She was as aloof as Alistair, if not more so.

My hand twitched and fidgeted on my wife's shoulder. She brought it down and kissed it before putting it in her lap. "Something on your mind?" she asked quietly. There was enough conversation going on around us where I was reasonably certain we wouldn't be overheard.

"I want to go out and look for Alistair. And your mom. I feel like it's my responsibility to do both of those things, and I'm stuck at home while everyone else is helping." It all came out in one breath and I felt deflated.

Lisbeth smiled and kissed my hand again. "You're a little moody lately. Is it that time of the month?" I scowled and tried to take my hand away from her, but she held on fast, giggling in her cute way until I pulled her onto my lap.

"*Touché*," I conceded. "I am feeling a bit moony. Things might get hairy later." She giggled again and snuggled closer to me. "Sorry. I feel like I've been super whiny lately."

"You forget," she said, sitting up to look at me. "I know you. And I know behavior. You're not upset about what you say you're upset about. It's just piling on top of the real issue."

My fingers started absently unraveling the braid I'd made in her hair. "And that is?"

Her hand went up to play with my hair too. "We had peace for decades, and during that peace, we ignored the real problems. It's a vampire thing. If the danger is not right in our faces, it might as well be forgotten." She leaned in and kissed me on the cheek before resting her head there. "You can't lay the blame on yourself. We all did this, and we will all work to make it right again."

I held her tightly against me as if she would blow away without my arms around her. "I love you so much."

"And I love you, you big hairy wolf."

We sat in the bus seat, cuddled together until the bus rolled into the airport parking lot. Lisbeth's body tensed, gripping my hand in wordless anxiety, and before I led her out of the bus, I planted a comforting kiss onto her cheek. Our large group entered the small airport and fanned out to the ticket kiosks before bag and security checks, and then traveling to their respective gates.

Lucas, Clara, Merrick, and Cameron were on different planes than Kitty, so we said our goodbyes to the other volunteers before walking the biker gang to their gate. Lisbeth's dad and aunt/step-mom hugged her for far longer than necessary, but she made no moves to pull away. Being away from them would be hard on her. Lucas released his daughter to let the women talk, approaching me with a serious expression.

"Son-in-law," he said with a nod, running his hand through his messy blonde hair before straightening his Napoleon looking jacket. Sometimes it felt like the less crazy he behaved, the crazier he looked. "Take care of my child. Thirty-five years together isn't enough to make up for four hundred years apart, and I intend to return in one piece to my little girl." He stepped into my offered hug, his head coming up to my chin, and he was by no means a small dude. I was simply ginormous. "I know I jest with you, werewolf, about my daughter leaving you, but I figure she has about as good a chance of surviving with you by her side as she does with the stoic one."

I pat his head, making sure not to sideswipe him like I wanted to. "Thanks, dad. That makes me feel better." Our hug started to last too long as well and I wiggled under his grasp. "Find Anastasia," I whispered to him. "She needs her mother."

Lucas sniffed and straightened. "Of course she does. You needn't ask. Clara and I do not intend to return without her."

He did the hair and jacket adjustment again as Clara came over to us.

"Knight," she said with a smile. Yesss, mother-in-law hugs. I was enveloped in the scent of baked bread and fresh plants for a few seconds before Lucas pulled his bride away from me, as usual. "Take care of them both. Give Jason my love."

"Always," I told her as I leaned in for a kiss on her cheek. Lucas whined, and Lisbeth cut him off with a light smack on his arm. Our goodbyes said, Lucas took Clara's hand and they waved as they disappeared into the crowd of humans. Cameron and Merrick were busy chatting with Kitty, and their goodbyes were swift and sweet. A hug, a kiss, a stiff warning for Cameron to take care of my sister, and they were gone too.

Kitty's group was ready to leave, and while they waited impatiently, she gave Lisbeth a very long hug. She was about to leave us for the first time. The thought was palpable for all three of us. I stood there, watching my women hug, and I found myself wondering how Kitty would say goodbye to me. A wave? A handshake? 'Bye Knight?' God, I was so self-ish. All I ever cared about was myself when it came to Kitty. When would she ever treat ME like her father? When would she call ME Dad? That's how I felt on the inside. On the outside, I converted that trepidation into respect for her space. It killed me, but I wanted her to be happy.

"Knight?" Kitty said. I realized I'd zoned out and didn't hear her talking to me. Her smile melted me, making me feel like a complete jerk. "Take care of Mom and Jason, okay? Tell Arthur I said he'd better keep you three safe." Her perfect little hand with her perfectly sharp and manicured fingernails curled up into a fist and she held it out for me.

A fist bump. Our *first* fist bump.

Bump.

She hugged Lisbeth again and was gone with the leather biker gang before I could lower my hand. Lisbeth looked over at me and at my still raised arm. Smiling, she walked to me and pulled me into a hug.

"You can put your hand down now."

"She fist bumped me. She's never fist bumped me." I might cry.

Lisbeth's head only reached my collarbone, like a short little pixie. She looked up at me with her chin against my chest. "Don't cry. Arthur's coming." I cleared my throat and put both arms around my wife as Arthur appeared in front of us.

Surprisingly, he had a sympathetic look for both me and my wife, so much so I thought he might hug us. *Did I want him to hug me?*

"Everyone is off on their flights, so we're good to go," he said, and shaking off my weird thoughts, we all left the airport back to the buses in the parking lot.

5

GOING FULL WOLF

*N*ightfall crept up like a slow crawl I couldn't avoid. My moodiness had a reason, and tonight I would shift into a wolf and do wolfy things like frolicking in the woods and crap. I left Lisbeth sated and sleeping in our bed before joining Jason in the living room. He was playing a game on the most current holographic gaming console, and looked up at me when I came in.

"Mom good?" he asked. He didn't like thinking she would be awake and worrying about us.

"She's asleep," I answered, picking up my bag. I had learned to leave my wife content and sleepy before going out for my moon escapades. It took a lot of my energy to sate my lioness, but I'd soon have more than enough to spare. My skin grew goosebumps in anticipation of what the night would bring.

"Good," Jason whispered as he was powering his console down. Flipping the lights off, we left the house as quietly as possible.

We walked down the street through our little village. A lot of our neighbors were still awake, and some waved to us as we walked by. I smelled barbeque and burning wood chips. My stomach growled at the thought of cooked meat.

"We'll be back to your mom before she knows it," I assured my son when I saw him looking back to our house.

"I hope my wife is like that someday," Jason said with a thoughtful smile that was far too mature for his age. "I want her to worry about me. Mom worries about all of us because she loves us. If my wife worries about me, I think that means she loves me."

I ruffled his dark hair and he dodged the attack. "Very insightful, my young padawan. And you're right. Women worry out of love. If she doesn't worry, she doesn't love you." We were reaching the end of the road and beyond it was dense forest.

"How many women were you with before mom?" Jason asked. He took a rubber band from his wrist to tie back his thick curls and I did the same with my long hair. The night air felt cold against my neck.

"A few. You can't really compare it, though. Once you find your mate, everything before fades away like it never mattered. If I saw those women today, they'd be invisible next to your mom."

Jason smiled at that and leaned in to whisper a secret.

"Mom told me about her first. She got jiggy with a French male prostitute."

I groaned and stepped into the forest. "She should've never told you that story. Remind me to complain to her later." Out of context, that story was hot because it was when she first felt desire, after over one hundred years of life. In context, it involved a prostitute. "Why were you two discussing that anyways? …. Are you… Are you getting jiggy with it?"

He snorted out a laugh. "No, dad. I'm just not a kid anymore. And mom wanted to tell me why you were different for her, how she knew you were her mate, even though she'd had lovers before. She didn't wait for love, but it wasn't the same before you."

"Your mom is a better woman than me, that's for sure," I said, my shoes crunching on the forest floor. "You make the choice that's right for you, son. We'll support it, no matter what. Boy. Girl. Non-binary. Android. Alien."

He laughed at me again. "C'mon dad, I'm being serious."

Deeper into the forest we went, and we fell silent walking beside each other. Jason didn't have to come with me on my moon trips, as he could change whenever he wanted to like Lycans could. He chose to be there by my side.

When Jason was born, we assumed he would need regular blood even if he was only half vampire, but my hybrid son was more human than vampire and only required blood if he was seriously injured. One time he'd broken his arm climbing a tree, and a quick bite into my shoulder fixed it in seconds. The fact that he preferred to only run with me was comforting. I'd always be here to give him blood if he got hurt.

Side by side, once we found a clearing we undressed down to our underwear and put our clothes into my bag.

"Shit, it's cold," Jason complained and gripped himself in a hug for warmth.

"Hey, we're werewolves, not swearwolves." But he was right, it was hella cold, even for us.

I hung my bag on a tree limb and glanced up at the sky. Not long now. I felt the moon coming, like an internal alarm inside my body. My skin felt itchy, and my muscles ached with need. Steam shot from my mouth in a ragged breath and I looked to the sky to see Her.

The moon.

She had me in her grip, and there would be no escape. Pain shot through every corner of my body. My joints cracked as my bones rearranged themselves. I tried not to cry out from the agony I was feeling. It was so hard. My hands grew into claws with a pain that felt like they were breaking in half. An audible groan escaped my lips as my face went white-hot and my snout formed. With a pop, my jaw snapped into place, and my transformation was complete. Panting, I looked up at the moon and howled, letting the pain out.

I was Hers once again.

Beside me, Jason had turned into his wolf form and he howled at the moon in harmony with me, echoing my mournful call. Jason was a bi-pedal wolf like me, but he was more wolf-like in appearance. He had more fur, bigger teeth, and his hands were more like paws. I had hoped he would resemble the wolf Lycans so they would accept him as part of their pack, but we were monsters in their eyes, no matter how much they liked us.

I turned to my pup and barked in signal before taking off into the forest. Jason followed me, step for step, under logs, and over creeks. Running helped take my mind off how much my body was throbbing with pain from the shift. The more I ran, the better I felt. Energy started surging through me, erasing how tired I'd felt before from loving on my wife. I kind of felt sad that she wasn't there because I was already starting to miss her. Maybe I'd bring her along the next time. It had been a while since she'd run with me during the full moon.

Jason was gaining speed on me, his body better suited to running on all fours than mine, but he made sure to stay on my flank in respect for his Alpha. That felt nice to say, that I was someone's Alpha. Maybe one day he and I would have another wolf running with us, whenever that fourth child from Lisbeth's dream arrived. Everything would turn out fine with baby number three, because the next baby was mine, and I found myself anticipating it with relish as we picked up speed.

An hour passed and we hadn't stopped running for anything. I felt free and happy. My chaotic emotions would even out now, thank god. No more whiny, moody Knight.

Back to manly me. We jumped over another river bank, sailing through the sky to land on the other side. My paws fell onto wet leaves and I skidded across the mud until I crashed into a tree, slamming my head against the trunk.

Jason was by my side in an instant, whining and sniffing at me for wounds. I felt a sharp pain in my side that was dulled by the adrenaline running through my system. The scent of blood drifted to my snout. My blood. I whined and I slumped to the ground, passing out.

When I woke up, I smelled Lisbeth nearby, and I felt her lifting me up in her arms. Leaves shuffled around her feet from Jason pacing in his wolf form.

"Have a fun night out with the boys?" she joked, her fingers pressing to my wounds. I whined and snorted at her. "Jason, stop pacing. Your father is okay. He's been in worse scrapes, believe me." The leaves stopped rustling and I heard Jason's tail swish back and forth on them. I opened my eyes and saw her beautiful, pale face in front of me. She was so gorgeous, like a goddess in Mount Olympus. People should erect monuments to her, and worship her hot body.

I think I was loopy from blood loss.

"Jason, go get your dad's bag." Jason scurried off, leaving us alone. If only I could kiss her with my dog lips. "Eww, Knight, seriously? We're not making out when you're in werewolf form." Oh, right, she could hear my thoughts with her vampire voodoo powers. "Yes, I can. And we're not making monuments for people to worship my hot body. Loopy from blood loss, indeed. You hit your head, don't be dramatic. And I don't have vampire voodoo powers." I chuckled through my snout, sounding like a bulldog coughing. Her fingers pressed into my side, feeling the wound. "You're healing fine, let's get you up." *Thanks for coming, love.* "Always," she said with a smile and helped me stand on my hind legs. "You're lucky I can still walk after earlier." I held out a paw for a high five but she narrowed her eyes at me. "I'm not high fiving that." *Whine.*

Standing in my wolf form, Lisbeth's head barely reached the top of my stomach. I leaned down and gave her a practiced kiss on the cheek with my dog-like lips. She put her arms around my neck and I lifted her up like she weighed nothing.

Mine.

"Yes, I know." She squeezed me harder and took a deep contented breath. "Mine." Lifting her head up, she brushed her nose against my wet dog snout. "I'm glad you're okay." Footsteps approached, it was Jason with my bag across his hairy shoulders. "Thank you, baby," Lisbeth told him. She took the bag and ruffled Jason's furry head, scratching behind his ears and making his foot pump up and down with his scratch reflex. He licked her hand appreciatively when she finished.

Can I has ear scratchies?

She rolled her eyes with a smile. "Yes, you big baby." Her fingers found the spot behind my ears I liked her to scratch, and my foot pumped up and down too.

Jason snorted at us, doggie language for 'get a room.' I

growled at him in a friendly manner and launched myself at him for some father-son wrestling. We nibbled at each other and fought to keep the other pinned while Lisbeth watched. My animal side felt the need to show her my strength as her mate, but I held back to make sure Jason stayed safe.

Finished playing, I jumped at Lisbeth and landed in front of her with a huff. She climbed on my back and I took off into the forest with our son behind me.

The moonlight eventually gave way to dawn, and Lisbeth took the small tent out of my bag for us to get inside after we were all human again. We crashed on the tent floor and instantly fell asleep. It was noon before I woke up. I'd somehow ended up on the opposite side of the tent than my wife, our son stretched out between us. Her purple eyes fluttered open and she smiled at me from behind Jason's sleeping form.

'Morning,' she said inside my mind. Her gaze turned to Jason and she reached out a hand to stroke his cheek and smooth his hair, leaning in to kiss his forehead. He stirred but didn't wake up, and scooted over to put his arms around her waist, resting his head against her breast as he'd done when he was a child. She kissed him again, holding our son close to her. *'Come here.'* Moving closer, I snuck a kiss on her lips and got in on that family cuddle. *'I love you.'* She shut her eyes and started nodding off again, wrapped in mine and Jason's arms.

I love you too.

6

THE EPIDEMIC BEGINS

*O*ur little group didn't make it back to the village until the full moon was over. We slept during the day and ran all night. Three days later, we emerged from the forest and did a walk of shame down the street in our muddy clothes to our yellow house. Jason took his shoes off and waved a hand behind him as he shuffled to his bathroom for a shower, yawning loudly. Lisbeth came up behind me for a hug and she yawned too.

"Such a bad dad, keeping us up all night," she joked sleepily. "Not my preferred reason to stay up."

"Mine either," I told her through my hoarse vocal cords. I was too tired for dirty jokes. "Shower, then sleep." She nodded and followed me to our bathroom to clean up four days of filth. We used half a bottle of liquid soap before our skin was sparkly clean. I stayed under the water a little longer and kissed her tenderly before she stepped out to put on one of our fluffy robes.

My ears pricked when I heard a knock at the door. Arthur.

"I got it," she shouted over the water and left the room.

I felt like I'd just done a juice cleanse, as if my entire body had been on edge and now I was finally relaxed. The water ran on my face, washing away the turmoil. Maybe it would wash away those weird thoughts I kept having about Arthur.

Lisbeth's small knuckles rapped on the bathroom door, interrupting my shower musings. "Knight, we need you." I twisted the shower handle, cutting off the water spray, and left the shower, grabbing a robe and putting it on before leaving the bathroom.

Arthur stood in the living room with Lisbeth next to him, and she held out a hand for me to take when I approached them.

"What's up?" I asked him, the look on his face setting my skin ablaze with dread.

"One of the teams we sent out went dark," he said grimly. Hell, even he couldn't mask the emotion behind the words. "It wasn't any of your family's groups." The air in my lungs expelled with a sigh of relief.

"Where were they?" I asked, squeezing Lisbeth's hand.

"We sent them to search Egypt and the surrounding countries, but they hadn't made it there before communication stopped. I estimate they were somewhere around Italy."

Lisbeth let go of my hand to grip the collar of her robe, as if it would shield her from all of this. "So Alistair is in Italy?"

Arthur shook his head, eyeing her like he wanted to reach out a hand and rub her shoulder, or anything to comfort her. "We don't know that yet. We'd have to re-route another group to check, but there's a chance they could also go dark from whatever got the first group."

"And then we'd never know for sure," I affirmed.

"Alistair isn't the only psycho out there," Arthur pointed out with a nod to me. "Plus some of the packs still aren't on our side, even after the alliance was made."

Leaning against the couch, Lisbeth fluffed up the top of her wet hair in thought. "I'm not sure what we can do at this point. We only have half the committee here. We can't make big decisions without everyone represented."

Arthur's holo-phone beeped and he flicked his wrist to answer it. "Report," he said into the microphone. I heard bits of the other person talking, a hurried message in a language I didn't understand, and Lisbeth's body tensed up as she eavesdropped. Apparently, she spoke the language, and it wasn't good news. "Wait for my orders," Arthur told the person and hung up. He gave a grave look to Lisbeth before turning his gaze to me. "Another team went dark. They were in Australia."

I ran both hands through my dark, wet hair to calm myself. "Dude can't be in two places at once."

Lisbeth gripped her neckline tighter. "I'm not making

plans wearing a robe. Brb." She left the room quickly, leaving me with Arthur.

I leveled him with as serious a look as I could muster, and he met it with his own. "Bring Kitty back here *now*," I told him. "I know you don't take orders from me, and that's fine, but do it for her."

"I'm surprised you think you have to ask. I already messaged Kitty's team before I got here. You should get dressed too."

I saluted him with two fingers on the side of my head and passed Lisbeth on my way out. She was already dressed in a blue cocktail number, complete with heels and jewelry. She always looked classic, and crazy beautiful. I kissed her and quickly closed our bedroom door before pulling on a pair of jeans and a t-shirt. Jason had joined the group when I emerged again, and Lisbeth was holding his hand, her face paler than usual.

Jason looked worried when he caught my eye. "Is Kitty okay?"

Lisbeth sniffed as quietly as she could. "Kitty is fine. We're all fine. Let's go to the meeting hall and see what's happening." Still holding Jason's hand, she marched out the door with all of us behind her, her heels clicking on the pavement. I allowed myself five seconds to appreciate the view of her walking in front of me. More than that felt wrong, considering the circumstances.

We burst through the meeting room doors like Aragorn

in The Two Towers. Hades and Balthazar were at the committee table and they hopped up when they saw us.

"Another one went dark?" Hades asked. I almost panicked, but I realized he was asking about the second group Arthur had mentioned before.

Arthur stomped up the steps to the table and shoved open a laptop before typing furiously at the keys. "All teams are being recalled until we find out what's happening." He typed more and lifted his eyes for a few seconds to where Lisbeth was, hugging Balthazar tightly. "Your parents are refusing to return."

She froze in the hug and slowly set her feet back to the ground. "I know. They're looking for Anastasia." Arthur made a noise that almost sounded like a groan. Hades wasn't quite that subtle.

"They can't bring that *murderer* here!" he bellowed, puffing up like a white balloon wearing coattails. "We pardoned your father and his bride, but I draw the line at your treacherous mother."

Lisbeth turned from Balthazar and leveled Hades with her serious face. No one could match her serious face. "If it wasn't for my mother, we'd all be dead. Deny it. *I dare you.*"

He withered under her ire and looked away. "The fact..." His voice cracked. "The fact remains that someone, or some*thing*, is killing our people. What if your mother went cray cray again? How do we know it's not her?" Hades saying 'cray cray' was worse than his ghastly fashion statements.

"I highly doubt this is one person," Arthur interjected

from his laptop. He straightened and opened his holo-phone to text really fast. "Another team went dark. Brazil. That makes three."

"Mom," Jason said quietly, brokenly, and not even Arthur was exempt from a reaction to it.

Lisbeth reached for his hand again, keeping her face very still. She was holding it together for his sake. "Kitty is in Canada. She's fine."

"Your family isn't more important than others," Hades huffed, pulling at his vest.

Lisbeth poked a finger at him. "You hush. My son is worried about his sister, and you're not helping." She turned to Arthur who was still typing away at his holo-phone, ignoring her just enough where she looked pissed. "I need answers, Arthur. I need them now."

"Apologies," he said, switching back to the laptop. "I have nothing yet."

Lisbeth sighed and pulled her holo-phone up. She typed with one hand, the other still holding Jason's, and then flicked her wrist to turn the holographic projection off. "I need to drink. Can we?" She motioned to me and I nodded back. Holding a hand out, I walked her to her office, closing the door behind us. She put her arms around my neck as soon as we were alone and held me close for several minutes. I wrapped her in my arms, felt her breathing become ragged with sobs. She sniffed, trying to hold back tears of worry. "If a leaf hit me right now, I'd fall into a thousand pieces."

"Putting you back together would be the best jigsaw

puzzle ever." She shook against me with laughter, but it didn't last long. I stroked her hair and lifted her chin up to kiss her lips. Neither of us was in the mood for passion, we just needed the intimacy of each other's touch. A reminder that we weren't alone. One more kiss and she had her arms around my neck again. "You need to drink."

She shook her head. "I can't, I'm not thirsty."

"For Jason."

Groaning, she loosened her grip on me and sank her teeth into my neck with a pop. Godddd, that pleasure-pain. It felt weird to actually love it, but I did. Her fangs retracted and she licked my neck to clean it up before her plump lips sucked my skin in a kiss and I had to pull her away.

"Woman," I admonished. "Totally hot. Not the right time."

"Sorry," she said with a smile. "I forgot where I was for a few seconds. You're just so devastatingly attractive." Her smile faded quickly when she remembered why we were there. "Let's go."

Lisbeth's furious texting was apparently ordering takeout because Jason was paying for it when we came back into the meeting room. There was fried chicken, mashed potatoes, coleslaw, biscuits, and hush puppies. Nothing like Southern food to make you forget your troubles. Even Hades was interested in snagging a plate.

We stayed there all afternoon but Arthur had no new

information for us, so we went home to sleep. Sleep was a relative term because none of us could relax enough to nod off, and eventually, we sat in the living room on the couch, all three of us, watching Star Trek: The Next Generation. By the cock crow, we'd all managed to slip into a doze that was interrupted by furious pounding on the front door.

Lisbeth groaned, let slip a few choice words, and stumbled over to the door to un-click the security bolts. Arthur came in like a hurricane and immediately grabbed the remote from my sleepy hand.

"Hey, man. My house, my remote," I complained drowsily, wiping my eyes with my fingers.

"Shut up," he ordered frostily and clicked the buttons on the remote until it switched off Netflix and onto the cable channels.

Lisbeth was the frosty one now, about to go full blizzard on his ass. "Do *not* talk to him like that. I don't care what's happening out there."

"You shut up too," he ground out, his words like a slap in the face. "How do I get it to show the effing Weather Channel?" He didn't use the word 'effing,' I'll say that much. Lisbeth had switched from pissed off to worried, and she locked eyes with me. Something was wrong. Arthur would never behave like this unless something was wrong. Like catastrophic wrong. The sky is falling wrong.

Jason stole the remote from Arthur and quickly switched it to the Weather Channel with little effort. "You know my mom is going to rip you a new one for talking to her like that." His smirk died when he saw what was on the screen.

A female news reporter was sitting at a desk with a stack of papers in front of her. "Authorities are calling this the worst epidemic in over a century, spanning all corners of the globe. Symptoms of this mystery disease include cold skin, manic behavior, and an unnatural surge in strength. Those affected are being restrained in order for doctors to treat them. We urge everyone to stay in their homes and try to get anyone affected by this disease to a hospital as soon as possible. We're now going live to our reporter on location for more insight on this epidemic."

Lisbeth wordlessly held her hand out for the remote and muted the television as soon as Jason gave it to her. We watched footage of the diseased humans restrained in hospital beds, fighting with everything they had to get free. A doctor pointed towards one human's mouth and showed the beginnings of fangs growing on the canine teeth. The screen switched back to the newscaster and Lisbeth turned the sound up again.

"No word yet on what this disease is, but doctors are working on a cure, and remain hopeful to get the affected back on their feet as soon as they can. Coming up next, how hurricanes affect the weather." Lisbeth clicked the television off and dropped the remote onto the carpet.

"That wasn't a disease," Jason said, almost phrasing it as a question.

"No," Arthur confirmed grimly. "That's the early stages of

creating a drone. Somehow it's not happening instantaneously like it's supposed to. The humans are turning into vampires, and if they aren't given human blood at the moment of turning, they'll go insane. They'll kill anything in sight with a pulse."

"They can't be turning... they can't..." Lisbeth wrapped her hands around the back of her neck, pacing the floor slightly in her worry. "How? Is someone biting them? Dropping blood in the water supply? I've seen it happen."

"I have as well. But even those humans turned the instant the vampire blood touched their lips," Arthur said, running his hand over his stubble.

"If it's Alistair, he's an Alchemist," Jason said, making us look over at him. "He'd have figured out how to prolong the turning. Maybe that's why he made that drone we found?"

"Genius," I praised, and reached a hand out for a fist bump, which he accepted. "What's our next move, team vamp-wolf-vae?"

"I'm not calling us that," Arthur protested with a grumpy sigh.

"I have an idea," Lisbeth offered, her face pinched in worry. "And none of you will like it."

I raised my eyebrows at her. "Ooo, do tell."

"Town meeting."

"You're right, I hate town meetings," Arthur said.

She shook her head at him. "Nope. That's not the part you won't like. Let's round up the troops."

Half an hour later, everyone from our village that hadn't left to search for Alistair was sitting in the meeting hall, waiting for Lisbeth's plan that she insisted we would hate. When everyone had found a seat and quieted down, Lisbeth stood up at the front of the stage, away from the committee table where the remaining members sat. Jason was sitting in for Kitty, and a silver-haired Alexander sat in for Jamie. The human spot remained empty without Clara.

"Good morning, everyone," Lisbeth opened. "I'm sure you've seen the news. The humans are fighting an epidemic, only it's not a disease. It's humans slowly turning into vampires. We suspect the difference in the change is because of Alistair. He's finally made his move to get revenge for what we did to him." She hesitated and fiddled her fingers together, Arthur and I sharing a mutual look of concern over her behavior. "I have a proposal. I can promise you that no one here will agree with me, but I urge you to understand that this is the only course of action that I believe can change the outcome of this situation for the better."

"Has the committee discussed this?" someone asked in the crowd.

Lisbeth shook her head and twisted her fingers more. "No. I didn't bring this to the committee first, because I wanted everyone to be aware of this before it is discussed and voted on."

I sent out a thought to her. *'Tell me first. It'll be easier.'* I saw her flinch slightly but she didn't answer me.

"The only way we can salvage this epidemic of mass turning is..." She gulped.

'Lis, please.'

Resolved, she raised her head. "We have to go public."

7

DRASTIC MEASURES

The outrage that erupted in that room after Lisbeth said those five words was indescribable. The shouting, the panic, and the finger-pointing. Lisbeth stood still through it all, her hands turning red from the constant twisting and turning. Arthur hopped up onto the stage to stand beside her to try and quiet the crowd, but it was no use. They were outraged, and no amount of shushing would shut them up.

I felt Lisbeth send a thought to me.

'Do you hate me?'

My heart broke into a thousand pieces. She actually thought that I'd be mad at her for this. If I truly thought it over, this probably was a last-ditch plan, but I didn't know of any other options. I shot from my chair and walked across the red-carpeted stage to stand beside my wife.

"Shut your pieholes and sit the eff down!" I shouted at the top of my lungs. While the room quieted, I took Lisbeth's swollen hand. "The committee is going to discuss this down the hall. We ask you to please stay here and wait for us to finish."

I heard Jason whisper, "Title of your sex tape." I snapped a finger at him and led the committee to Lisbeth's office.

"This is madness," Hades said when the door had shut behind us.

"I'm pretty sure this is Sparta," I muttered, because I couldn't help myself. He leveled me with a glare and ran his fingers through his oily red locks.

"We have remained in hiding for thousands of years, and this wet-nosed female thinks she can undo that? Poppycock."

"I suggest you chill out, Nosferatu," I ordered and flicked a finger to him in warning.

"I agree with the plan," Alexander said suddenly. He had found a chair to sit in and was leaning forward with his elbows on his knees.

Hades crossed his arms over his chest. "Well, that's two votes for insanity."

Balthazar was perched on the desk, legs crossed effortlessly like this was a Sunday picnic. "There are no other viable options?" He looked at Arthur for confirmation. The room held its breath for the stoic warrior to speak his peace. He chewed on it for longer than I would've thought necessary, even for this situation. Then his icy blue eyes found me.

"What do you think?"

Arthur. Asking for *my* opinion. Someone get the paddles, I'm going into shock.

I looked down at my doe-eyed wife, so afraid that she would lose me with this decision. I kissed her on the head to comfort her and she held onto my waist tightly, like I was going to float away if she didn't.

"This is for the humans?" I asked her.

She nodded against my stomach. "Yes. If we don't act fast, the humans might suffer a catastrophic population failure. We can't exist without them."

"So they get reduced in number, big deal," Hades reasoned, being as unhelpful as possible. "We can survive."

"It's not just that," she countered. "Say they start to hunt the drones. They develop a test to see if anyone is affected. A test that vampires won't pass. They'll shoot us on sight."

Arthur stroked his chin and studied the ceiling in thought. "But if we come forward first, and help the humans prevent the drones from turning as much as possible, they'll view us as allies. They'll hunt the drones, but not us."

"Exactly," Lisbeth affirmed. Hades muttered under his breath some very unkind things. I signaled with my fingers that I was watching him.

"There are no other options," Arthur told Balthazar, and all of us as well.

Balthazar uncrossed his legs and plopped his feet down onto the carpet. "That settles it. I vote yes."

"Me too," Jason said.

"Humph, he's not even an official member," Hades complained.

"I vote yes too," I echoed. "Five against one."

Lisbeth was chewing her lip now, and I was starting to smell her blood. "They won't like it."

"Of course they won't," Hades commented dryly. "Our way of life will end. Nothing will be certain. If they don't unseat all of us over this, I will be shockingly surprised."

"They can't unseat me," I pointed out, not that it helped.

Hades rolled his eyes. "I'm sure they will find a way if they're pissed enough." He straightened his black jacket. "Let's go break the news, and pray we leave with our heads attached."

To put it mildly, the crowd didn't take it well when we stood on the stage and told them that a vote of five to one had decided we would go public to the humans.

"I will not be party to this blasphemy," a vampire shouted.

"The agreement of this committee is that you would represent us fairly, and if we thought you were misrepresenting us, we could replace you," another yelled out, his ugly, pale finger pointed at my wife. "I vote we replace this traitorous woman, and leave her in the gutter like her harlot mother!"

And like that, the crowd turned ugly.

Funny how we always feared humans taking up their pitchforks and trying to burn us to the ground when we should've feared our own kind doing just that. The people we'd sworn to protect and fought for with our lives no longer wanted us to help them. The vampires replaced Lisbeth on the committee, and the Lycans quickly did the same with myself and Alexander.

To make matters worse, they locked us inside our house to make sure we wouldn't go public to the humans. They would've locked us in prison, but we didn't have jail cells anymore.

An hour into our imprisonment, Alexander was lying down in Kitty's room, I sat at the kitchen table with Balthazar, Arthur was pacing the carpet raw, and Lisbeth was on the couch with Jason, petting his hair so he'd fall asleep. She had the television tuned to news coverage about the plague with the volume on mute. Every hour the news got more and more heated, and the epidemic was the only thing discussed on the air.

"It's getting worse," Balthazar commented, drumming his fingers on the table.

"And we're stuck in here like criminals," Arthur ground out. He didn't like being caged. Score for finding his pressure point, though.

Lisbeth kissed Jason's head and left him on the couch. "If we want to go forward with the plan, we have to do something drastic." Arthur stopped pacing, turning to her. "We have to go rogue and break vampire law."

"Oh *hell* no," he muttered. "I am not doing that. I literally hunted our kind for that. *Literally.*"

"Yeah," she said with a smile, batting her eyelashes at him. "And now you work for me. And I say you're not allowed to hunt me for it. Checkmate." He swore under his breath. "Also," she added, turning her grin on me. "They made one fatal error locking us all in here. They let me keep my food supply. No offense, honey."

"None taken."

"A quick binge and I'll be able to control anyone we encounter long enough for us to leave. As long as you're okay with it, dear."

I shrugged. It would never be like the first time she blood binged. She'd never go too far again. "Fine by me."

"Part two of the plan." She turned to Balthazar. "We're outing supernatural beings to humans. Humans with guns, and bombs, and happy trigger fingers. I want my son nowhere near this. Balthazar, I'm asking you to take him far away from here. If we never come back, you have to be his guardian."

"I recall the last time you asked me to take a child away for safety you offered to let me marry a sexy librarian. Is that part of this deal too?" Balthazar smiled and drummed his fingers against each other. She glared, asking him to be serious. "What's wrong with the other wolf? Alexander? Shouldn't the boy be raised by his own kind?"

"It would be ideal, but we need him to come with us. I can flash fang all I want to the humans and they might not believe me, but a man turning into a wolf will be hard to ignore."

Balthazar sighed in defeat. "As long as Knight is fine with it, I will agree. The boy will be safe with me." He looked at me, and I nodded. He wouldn't have been my first choice to raise Jason, but considering the circumstances, he would do his best. "Very well. I own a secret island. We'll be safe there."

"A secret island where?" Arthur asked curiously.

"Secret as in secret, icy one." Balthazar stood and kissed Lisbeth reverently on the forehead. "I'll pack my bag, I suggest the boy does the same. We will await your orders."

"On it," Jason said from the couch, apparently not as asleep as we'd thought. "Also totes going to drive him insane. Just saying. Can I bring my console?"

Balthazar looked like he was already regretting this. "The flashy game thing? Fine. As long as you never say you're bored." Jason got up and gathered his console with the controller and wires and went to his room to pack a bag with Balthazar following behind him.

"I regret everything," Lisbeth groaned, rolling her eyes to the ceiling.

"He'll keep the boy safe," Arthur said as he tried to comfort her, still standing too far away for it to be effective.

"He's right, babe. Balthazar is the best choice for the options we have." I saw Alexander come out of Kitty's room and stretch his arms above his head.

"What are we doing?" he asked with a yawn. Thirty-five years had done a number on him. Lycans aged slower than humans, but they still aged. He'd already been sixty, in age at least, when Lisbeth met him, and now he actually looked sixty, decades later. His black hair was completely silver, he had wrinkles, and he was already regretting the pain of shifting so much that he was considering stopping.

"Going rogue," I answered with a smile.

He yawned again. "Cool. Can I eat something first?" I nodded and he disappeared into the kitchen.

While he heated up leftovers, we went to our bedroom to pack a bag of essentials. Mine was mostly clothes, my hand-held gaming console, and a few keepsakes. It wasn't clear if we'd be able to return to our home after this, and I didn't want to leave anything precious behind. Out of the corner of my eye, I watched Lisbeth put her digital book reader into her backpack, along with the small baby keepsakes box she had with the silver rattles and wooden crosses from our children's christenings. Her most precious possessions. She'd never bring them if she thought we were coming back.

I leaned over to her on the other side of our bed and kissed her forehead, wanting nothing more than to hold her close until this was all over. She gave me a quick smile and went back to putting her small stack of first edition books on top of the box. I zipped up my bag and slung it over my shoulder as she picked up a small pile of clothes and shoved it in before zipping up her backpack and putting it on.

"It was nice, having my own house," I said quietly, looking around at the custom crown molding and the crisp wall-paper with little birds on it. Lisbeth loved this house. She sniffed, pretending there was dust in the air, wiped her eyes where she thought I couldn't see, and picked up one last thing to bring: her Bathory necklace. She clasped it behind her neck and flipped the pendant over to show her crest.

"Let's go."

When we were all packed and ready, Lisbeth drank deeply from my neck with Arthur's hand on her shoulder to judge when she should stop. I needed enough blood to still be of some use while my body made more. A noise escaped my lips as she drank, and let's just say I didn't like my son hearing me make that sound. When Arthur squeezed her shoulder, she licked my skin clean and moved away from me.

"Ready?" she asked everyone. We nodded, and she kicked open the front door, shattering the wood and destroying any barriers our kinsmen had put in front of it. Two guards were outside the door, and Lisbeth raised her hands at them. "*Sleep*," she commanded. They flopped to the ground like gummy worms.

Arthur raced off to our garage and ripped open the locked garage door with his bare hand. I heard the blaring roar of him starting my jeep engine, but his escape from the garage was blocked by more guards. Dozens of them appeared and they were intent on stopping us. Lisbeth raised both hands, focusing so hard I saw veins bulging in her face. Most of the guards fell asleep and we quickly dispatched the rest with blows to the head. I was there to catch Lisbeth when she went limp from the exertion. I threw her arm over my shoulder and carried her to my jeep.

Balthazar drove up in his black sports car that probably costed more than our entire house. He rolled the window down and motioned for Jason to get in. Jason came to where we stood behind my jeep and hugged us tightly. Lisbeth was on the verge of passing out, but she managed to find more than a few tears for him.

I lost count of how many times we all said I love you in that moment. We kissed our wet cheeks, hugged our son so tight we heard bones creak, and wished there was another way. The human world would never understand what we did for them in the shadows.

Lisbeth gasped in a breath and wiped Jason's cheeks again. "If we make it out, we'll find you and Kitty. I promise." Jason nodded and sniffed to hold back more tears. "Go. Go with Balthazar. If I have to say goodbye again, I won't survive." Our son nodded and was off to the black car that pulled away with a screech, taking him away from us. My wife slumped against me, her head dipped so low I thought she had lost consciousness.

"Let's go before more of them come," Arthur shouted, just as we heard more of our kind moving towards us. I lifted my wife into the vehicle and jumped up to sit next to her before thumping my hand on the metal side, Arthur accelerating instantly down the road.

One arm around my wife, the other holding onto one of

the metal bars on the back of my jeep, I watched our city get further and further away. Our home would be forever lost to us now.

Lisbeth eventually turned and slid into the backseat, tugging on me to do the same. Alexander and Arthur were silent in the front seat, and every so often Arthur would look through the rearview mirror to check on Lisbeth. She sat next to me, her face blank and her body frozen.

A lump came to my throat when I realized she was reminding me of Anastasia. Anastasia who had died inside when she lost one child. Lisbeth had just lost two. Ignoring safety laws, I gently picked her up and put her on my lap to straddle me. Her head lowered to my collarbone and her arms came up around my neck. I stroked her hair, planted kisses on her head, but she didn't respond. I met Arthur's eyes in the mirror and a look passed between us, one that spoke more volumes than words, and I'd never felt so close to him before then.

'Don't leave me,' I sent to her.

Her head lifted and she looked into my eyes, with a sorrow so great on her face that I couldn't bear it. She leaned in for a soft kiss, her lip quivering ever so slightly, and I wanted for all the world to show her with every intimate detail that I was there for her, but we weren't alone. Her lips were salty when she kissed me one last time and laid her head back on my shoulder. I tried not to notice when the spot of my shirt underneath her head grew more and more wet.

8

GENERAL LANCASTER

*A*rthur drove all night, and when we woke up in the back seat, in front of us was the back of the iconic White House.

I yawned and tried not to move too much so Lisbeth could sleep more in my lap. "How long have we been here?"

"Couple hours," Arthur answered. It was not lost on me how his body was turned in the driver's seat so he had a clear view of Lisbeth's sleeping form. I smelled take out and searched around for food. Arthur immediately handed me two wrapped burgers. "They're both for you." I smiled because I would've definitely set one aside for my wife, and he knew me well enough to know that. I ate the first burger one-handed, my other hand around Lisbeth's waist. Every few bites, I checked on her to see if I'd disturbed her but she remained in a blissful slumber. When the second burger was in my stomach, Arthur handed me a drink and I sipped it appreciatively. "Wake her up."

"Dude, do you have a death wish? You never wake this one up when she's sleeping."

"Claws and fangs?" Alexander guessed, grinning. I mimicked what waking her up looked like with a very scary face and baring my free hand like I was about to slice him up. He laughed so loud I thought she would wake up from it, but she remained asleep.

"Put your drink down," Arthur said quietly. I did so, eyebrow raised. "Sorry not sorry." He banged his hand on the jeep horn, honking loudly enough to wake the dead, which is exactly what it did. Lisbeth shot awake, claws and fangs out, and just barely managed to not cut me in her rage attack. I couldn't say the same for my jacket. Arthur, the tosser, was *laughing his ass off* in the front seat, chorused by Alexander chortling so hard he started a coughing fit.

"*I will literally murder you,*" Lisbeth ground out in my face. "Not you, dear." She kissed me on the cheek. "The wanker in the front seat. *Dead.*"

He stopped laughing instantly and went back to his normal blankness. "I'm not a wanker."

"Totally a wanker," she argued. "Where's my food?" He handed her a burger and she started biting into it when Arthur got out of the jeep.

"We have an appointment with the President," he said casually like it was a doctor appointment. "We'll be late." Alexander got out as well and they both brought their bags with them. I hopped out the back of the jeep, putting my bag on, while Lisbeth climbed out and put hers on one-handed, the other full of burger.

"How'd you swing that?" she asked, mouth full of food. Arthur didn't respond, and that usually meant he didn't want us to know the answer. She licked her fingers and rolled her eyes. "Brick wall. All day, every day." Her holo-phone buzzed and she motioned for me to take it from her jeans pocket so she could keep eating. I put the phone on my wrist and pressed the button to open a text.

"It's a text from Olivier," I told her. "It says, '*Heard you were arrested and then you broke out of jail. Ha ha ha, ha ha ha, laughing so hard I cried emoji. Also p.s. Your Jimmy Choos are mine. Hashtag no regrets.*'" Lisbeth laughed, coughing up some food in the process. The holo-phone buzzed again and another text from Olivier came up. "She also says, '*Agree with the plan. Tell us where to meet you.*'"

"I'll answer," Arthur offered, and pulled his holo-phone up to text her back. Lisbeth finished her food just as we reached the back fence. Secret Service agents stood at attention and gave us a once over before approaching Arthur. He leveled them with an authoritative look. "We're here to see the President. General Arthur Lancaster reporting in."

General?

The SS agents stepped away to call it in and authenticate our arrival, so I leaned into Arthur. "General?" I hissed, holding in a laugh. "Nice swing. Did you get that title just for this?"

Arthur side-eyed me with a frown. "No. I'm actually a General. For reals," he added sarcastically.

Lisbeth made a noise like she was trying not to giggle. "I definitely don't pay you enough, General Lancaster."

"Okay, calm down," Arthur ground out, elbowing her in the side. "They needed a last name, and I gave them one. Don't be a child. Plus may I point out, you also have a last name."

She stuck her tongue out at him and he stared at it, probably contemplating biting it to shut her up. "Yes, because my human grandmother acknowledged her illegitimate vampire child. That's never happened before."

The SS agents came back and gave us the okay to come inside the fence. We followed one of them up to the back door where more security stood, and he opened it to let us in. Lisbeth eyed all the guns we were seeing with a wary glance.

"Right this way, General Lancaster," the agent said. He walked us past bag checks and the metal detector, down a small hallway and into The Green Room. The freaking Green Room.

Lisbeth groaned to herself, looking around at the décor. "And here I thought I'd never have to be in a green drawing room again. God hates me."

Alexander also looked around and made a face. "They definitely have vampiric taste. No offense."

Arthur and Lisbeth echoed, "None taken." I found a striped couch that looked older than me and laid on top of it.

Lisbeth hissed at me with wide eyes. "That's really old, stop lying on it like it's a futon!" My retort was cut short because the President entered the room. He was about as old as Alexander looked, and he had on a dark blue suit. I'd always gotten a nice Grandpa vibe from him when I saw him on television. In person, I still felt that.

"General Lancaster," he said with a smile to Arthur. "How nice to see you again. When you called asking for a meeting, I admit I was a bit anxious, especially considering the epidemic going on out there. You only hear from General Lancaster when there's an emergency."

How right he was.

"Mr. President, we have something very serious to discuss with you," Arthur told him. "It requires absolute privacy." He motioned to the SS agents standing at the door. The one standing closest to the President opened his mouth to say something like, *'No effing way,'* but the President held up his hand to silence everyone.

"Gentlemen, give us a few minutes." And like that, the room emptied of all but the five of us. "Sit. Let's talk." He motioned to a table with several chairs, and we pulled up more from around the room for everyone to have a place.

For the first time in my life, I watched vampires and Lycans tell a human what we were. Sure, we told companions and human mates what we were, but we gradually introduced the idea until it wasn't a shock. This time it was completely cold turkey and all on the table at once.

The President took it in stride, leading me to guess

maybe aliens were real and he'd encountered humanoid beings before. When we finished, he stood up and walked over to one of the large windows, as if the sunlight would help wash away what he'd just learned.

"I'll admit," he said finally. "I've had my suspicions about General Lancaster for many years." Oh hell. That could either be very good, or very very bad. "When I first met him, he introduced himself as the grandson of the man that fought beside my grandfather in World War I. My grandfather described a man that made it out of every battle with nary a scratch on him when the other men were torn to pieces. He made other claims, such as his friend would pick the battlefield for dying soldiers so he could do something odd to their neck. I was willing to let my grandfather's fantastical tales remain just that until I myself served with General Lancaster. Though I cannot boast such remarkable findings as him sucking a man's blood, through the years he's remained remarkably well preserved, among other things."

Lisbeth was giving Arthur some wicked side-eye during the President's speech. Boy had slipped up, and judging by his intense study of the crown molding, he knew it.

"You suspected General Lancaster of something, and stayed silent?" she asked the President, still glaring at Arthur.

"Accusing a decorated soldier of sucking blood and turning into a bat wouldn't be very beneficial to anyone," he chuckled.

"We don't turn into bats," Arthur muttered with a frown.

"My apologies. Still. I knew General Lancaster's character, and no man who fought as bravely as he would willingly harm us. Whatever he was, I knew I could trust him. I had no idea I would ever get an answer for my suspicions, but I am very glad that if there are other species on earth, they are willing to work with us to help save as many humans as possible." He turned back to us. "The press conference you requested is about to begin. I assume you will fully reveal yourselves to the public?" He tapped a finger to his tooth in example. We nodded. "Good. Once the conference is over, we will begin working on an alliance. No public feeding, signed consent, so on and so on. We can worry about the technicalities later, once your people elect delegates."

He led us out of the room and through more hallways, down some stairs, and over to the press briefing room. It was crowded with reporters and cameras, eager to get the scoop on the biggest story ever.

"Ladies and gentlemen," someone said into the microphone on the stage. "The President of the United States." Everyone clapped as we all stepped onto the stage behind the Big Man. He waved and smiled at everyone like it was a normal day with normal news. Flashbulbs went off left and right, and the camera in the center aisle moved closer to film us for live tv.

The President leaned into the microphone and stared straight at the camera in the middle aisle. "My fellow Americans." Oh god, why. It's 2053, think up a new opener, people. "In light of recent events involving the epidemic plaguing not just our nation but all around the globe, we have discovered some new information that will help eradicate this disease."

Something in the room was making me sweat. Was it hot in here? Someone, probably an intern judging by his outfit, was passing out water bottles to the press. Maybe the air conditioning had broken.

The President continued. "What I'm about to reveal to you might be a tad frightening, but I can assure you, the people on stage with me will not harm you." He motioned to Lisbeth and whispered into her ear when she approached. "Please introduce yourself."

Lisbeth took his place at the podium. "My name is Erzsébet Bathory. Yes, like the serial killer. I was born in 1603, I'm four hundred and fifty years old. I'm married, or bonded as we call it in my culture. I have two children, Kitty and Jason." The reporters were silent, most likely from confusion. Who was this crazy chick telling us she was four hundred and fifty years old? Lisbeth looked over at the President for instructions on what to do next, and he caught my eye to motion me forward.

I gave Lisbeth a kiss on the temple when I stood next to her at the podium. "My name is Jason Knight Trimble. I was born in 1842, I'm two hundred and eleven years old. I fought in the Civil War. This is my wife, Lisbeth. We were married thirty-five years ago. Best choice I ever made. That, and not buying an 8-track in the sixties, amirite?" The crowd remained confused, but a few took more pictures.

Alexander was next, and he squeezed in beside me. "My

name is Alexander Locklear. I was born in 1955, I am ninety-eight years old. I have three children, ten grandchildren, fifteen great-grandchildren, and two great-great-grandchildren. They're still babies."

Lastly, Arthur came up to Lisbeth's other side, sliding his hand into hers to steady her. "My name is General Arthur Lancaster. I earned my rank serving in both World Wars. I was born in 1770, I'm two hundred and eighty-three years old." The President whispered in his ear and Arthur leaned into the microphone. "I'm a vampire."

"Umm, same," Lisbeth said, chewing her lip.

"I'm a werewolf," I added. My pits were becoming bogs from the heat. Okay, someone had definitely turned on the heater. This was ridiculous.

"And I'm a Lycan. Slightly different than the werewolf," Alexander said with a grin.

A reporter on the first row looked like she thought we were having a laugh. "Is this a joke? Mr. President?" She picked up her bottle of water and took a swig, then fanned her blouse against the rising temperature of the room.

We made way for the President to stand between us. "This is not a joke. Miss Lisbeth, if you would."

She took a step back and met my eyes. I answered with a nod, so she moved to the right more for the humans to see her fully, Arthur's hand still clutching hers. She hissed and flung her other hand out to unfurl her claws, and her fangs dropped down, turning her eyes bright red. The crowd gasped appropriately, especially when Arthur did the same.

"Artifice! Special Effects!" the crowd cried, exactly how the humans had reacted at the circus.

The President held up a finger to shush them. He looked a little pale from seeing my wife looking all badass, but he was determined to be on our side. "Mr. Alexander?"

Alexander took one step to the side and started shifting into a wolf before the humans' eyes. I heard him groaning in pain while his bones cracked and rearranged themselves. He hadn't shifted in months, it must've felt like he was dying. Finished, he stood beside me, a very large, and very real wolf.

The crowd couldn't explain this away, and they started to panic. The President waved his hands to try and calm them.

"The vampires and Lycans are our allies. With their assistance, the epidemic will end."

No one was listening to him. He'd taken the news well. This room of reporters had no such plans. One of them tried to leave and ran into an SS agent who wrestled to keep her under control.

I can't really say how it happened, but I will say that I wish I could've reacted sooner. That one panicked woman wrestling with the SS agent elbowed him in the face, grabbed his gun, and fired at the stage.

9

ARTHUR CRIES

The shouting. The screaming. The blood. So much blood. The sweet metallic smell filled the air and suddenly the room stopped moving like Adam Sandler had hit the pause button.

Every human had fallen to the floor.

Lisbeth was by my side instantly, not noticing the stillness around us, she was too absorbed in trying to staunch the flow of blood on Alexander's furry body. The bullet had hit him square in the neck, and judging from the amount of blood coming from the wound, he wasn't going to survive it, even with his advanced healing.

"You'll be okay," she lied in a soothing tone, pressing her hands to the wound, covering herself with crimson blood. Alexander coughed and blood spurted out his wolfy mouth. "We need to stop the blood flow so he can heal." Her voice was breaking. She knew Alexander was beyond help, but she would fight for him until his chest stopped moving.

Arthur's hand touched my shoulder and I looked up to see his eyes trained on the crowd. The crowd that was slowly standing up from the carpet. "Knight, bring Lisbeth here," he whispered to me. She protested when I reached for her, and especially when Arthur put his hand over her mouth, holding her between our bodies. "No sudden movements." He slowly lowered his hand from her mouth once he knew she wouldn't cry out.

"What's happening?" she hissed, watching him closely.

His crystal eyes were trained on the crowd. "They've turned."

Oh shit.

Lisbeth stifled her reaction with a hand to her face. "All of them?" He nodded slowly. "How? There wasn't a drone in here to infect them."

I looked down at the humans and saw them moving ever so slowly towards us. One of them knocked over a bottle of water, the bottles I'd seen the skinny intern passing out. The label was a brand I'd never seen before. "The water," I said, pointing my finger just barely. "They were all drinking it."

"You're telling me Alistair found a way to turn humans through water without biting them first?" Lisbeth asked, her voice gaining pitch with each word. Arthur grabbed her wrist and made her step closer to the other side of the stage where the President stood, white-faced, staying as still as possible. I followed carefully behind them.

"Mr. President, I need you to move very slowly to that door over there," Arthur whispered carefully, his eyes trained on the horde.

"What about my men?" the President hissed. He looked about ready to pee himself.

Arthur shook his head just barely. "They drank the water too. I saw it. We're the only ones who didn't. We'll protect you, I promise. Just get to that door." With her right hand in Arthur's grip, Lisbeth reached back for me with her left, and I took it gladly, my sweaty palms almost too slippery to hold on. "Alexander." We didn't look behind us, but I could still hear Alexander's heart beating, getting slower and slower. "We have to leave you, I'm sorry. Don't make any noise or you'll trigger them. They're homing in on your blood right now as their thirst is rising."

Lisbeth sniffed quietly, trying her hardest to hold in the tears, but Arthur wouldn't meet her gaze. "We can't leave him."

Robotically, Arthur tugged her towards the door. "He's dying. If we try to move him, they'll attack us."

"We've fought off less than this and survived."

He turned his head back to her with a hiss. "Yes, when we had reinforcements, and we weren't trying to keep a human alive. For once in your life, *stop arguing with me and let me save your damn life.*"

Her eyebrows narrowed and she looked pissed enough to rage kill the entire room. "We're having words about this later." For once, I agreed with Arthur. The longer we stayed, the less chance we had of coming out alive.

"Let's go," I ordered her, and almost shoved her forward. "You can scold him when we're not about to die."

The President had reached the door, slowly turning the handle to be as quiet as possible. It creaked ever so slightly and the mob started making noises I didn't like. The ones on our side of the room were getting closer.

"Damn it," Arthur swore, pushing forward to push the door open. It triggered the crowd, and they raced forward to stop us and sink their teeth in our throats. Arthur shoved us all inside the doorway, jumping in at the last second with claws and teeth coming after him. Several had gotten a grip on his shirt and I scratched at them until they let go and the door shut with a slam. We pushed our bodies against it to hold it closed and it bumped from the strain of the humans trying to get to us. "This won't hold them for long," Arthur ground out, grunting from holding the door.

Lisbeth added her strength between us. "They were in the final stages of the turn. If they don't get human blood, they'll become drones."

My feet lost their hold with another push and I struggled to stay upright. "I don't see any blood available." God, they were strong. We could barely keep the door closed.

"Get the President to the jeep," Arthur ordered Lisbeth, and he pushed her with his hand before putting it back on the door.

"God, you're bossy," she muttered before walking over to

the President and slinging him over her shoulder. She met both of our eyes in turn, and I could tell she was afraid we wouldn't make it out of the building. "You'll follow?"

"As soon as you're clear," I promised her. She nodded, giving us both significant looks, and disappeared around the corner.

"Give her a few minutes, just in case," Arthur grunted. The door swung slightly and bumped back into the frame, the wood cracking with a sickening jolt. "Or not." He looked at me and nodded. "One. Two. Three." At three, we both pushed away from the door and started running in the direction Lisbeth had gone.

We found her on the lawn running towards the gate, still towing the President across her back. Before we'd gotten down the stairs, blood-crazed drones came from out of nowhere, rounding the corner of the building and going straight for her. There was no time to react, and both of us shouted her name before the monsters slammed into her like linebackers. The President went one way and she went another, her small body sailing through the air and landing with a smack several feet away.

She didn't get up.

I didn't think, I charged into the enemy lines like Wolverine, howling and tearing at anything my hands touched just to get closer to my wife. Arthur was beside me, claws and fangs out, and he tore into the drones with his teeth, ripping out pieces of their flesh. We turned them into ribbons. When there were no more left, we both ran to where Lisbeth still lay, unmoving.

Her skin was torn in so many places, I couldn't tell where they ended and she began. The drones had ripped her apart, just as we'd done to them. Thankfully they hadn't torn anything off. I wasn't in the mood to search for body parts. But they'd done major damage, and she was as still as I'd ever seen her. Still as if she was dead.

"*Lis,*" Arthur whimpered, his fingers running along the curves of her face, the look on his face of utter despair doing me in.

She couldn't leave me. I wasn't ready to lose her. I'd never be ready to lose her. Thirty-five years wasn't long enough. I needed her forever. I gave myself to her for forever, and I intended to have her for just as long, damn it!

"*Lisbeth,*" I cried out and picked her up to cradle her in my arms, Arthur's hands right there to assist. Her neck flopped unnaturally to the side, like a newborn baby. "Arthur, help me." My cheeks were wet and I could barely see from the tears. He gently lifted her head and put his ear to her breast. I smelled so much blood coming from her, I felt like I'd never wash the smell from my nose. Even as distracted as I was, I strained to hear the heartbeat he was trying to find.

Bump bump. Bump bump.

"Her neck is broken, but she's still got a heartbeat," Arthur said after several beats.

She wasn't dead yet. She wasn't gone for forever yet. I sobbed brokenly, freely, in front of the only man I trusted to see me that way. I knew he was feeling as much pain as I was, and somehow it made this more bearable, if that was possible. He helped fold her into my arms, making sure to keep her neck straight, and held me steady as I stood up. I nodded my chin over to where the President lay.

"He's dead?" I didn't want to take my attention from Lisbeth's heartbeat even for a second.

Bump bump. Bump bump.

Arthur looked over and sniffed a few times, not from tears, just smelling the air. "Yep. Nothing we can do. Let's go." He walked ahead of me to open the gate. Lisbeth didn't feel as warm as she usually did and her breathing slowed to a speed I didn't like. We rushed as fast as we could to the jeep. Once we reached it, something weird was happening. Every human nearby was lying on the ground, each one with a bottle of that water in their hands.

Arthur said a few words that would make a sailor blush and started the jeep. "Get in. They're all turning."

Alistair clearly believed in the phrase, 'Go big or go home.' He'd turned the entire White House in one fell swoop, and now the city was turning as well, all from bottles of water.

Quickly, but as gently as possible, I got in the front seat and held Lisbeth against me before buckling us both in. We sped out of the parking lot and onto the road, a road littered with car crashes. Arthur zigzagged through the road to avoid them.

Bump bump. Bump bump.

Keep beating, heart. Keep her alive.

We made it a few blocks before the bodies started getting up. "We have about five minutes before they go crazy," Arthur shouted over the car engine. "Once they're awake, if they don't get blood within about a minute, it's too late. The ones in the conference room went crazy from the smell of Alexander's blood. It sparked their thirst sooner."

Bump..... bump bump.

I buried my face in Lisbeth's hair, breathing in the scent of her. Blood stuck to my cheek. "Will she be okay?" I felt like a little boy asking if Daddy was coming back from getting ice cream.

Arthur's lips pressed together. "If we don't get out of this city alive, it won't matter." He slammed his foot into the gas pedal and we swerved to get on the freeway. "With drones on the loose, it probably would've been better to have a car with all the sides closed," he commented dryly.

I laughed brokenly. "I like to feel the wind in my hair."

He snorted. "You just like sticking your head out the window, admit it."

"Sh... shut up," I countered with a sniffle. Lisbeth's head lolled when we hit a bump and I fumbled to keep her upright. Arthur's hand came up to steady her, carefully putting her in my arms again.

Bump. .... Bump.

The cars on the freeway had drones struggling to get out of the doors, but most of the cars had crashed and the doors were too damaged to open.

"Why isn't her neck fixed yet?"

"Broken bones take a few hours to heal without feeding." I knew that, but I was impatient for her to not be hurt like this. If only I'd gone with her, then maybe I'd be the broken one and not her. I'd give anything to switch places with her.

Arthur swore, bringing me out of my thoughts, and I turned to find what he was seeing in the rear-view mirror.

An army of drones coming after us.

He turned off at an exit and swerved around more cars before finding a road that was mostly empty. Arthur sped the car up faster and faster until we were going the max speed on the speedometer, and the crowd started getting smaller. They couldn't match our velocity even with their enhanced speed.

"We're losing them," I said. Arthur nodded and continued going top speed, just in case. "We should go back home."

Bump.

He shook his head and picked at the leather steering wheel cover. "Drones or no drones, we went public. The humans saw it on a live broadcast. If we go back home, we'll be shot on sight for treason. We need to be as far away from humans and our own kind as possible right now."

"We have a cabin in the mountains. There are no humans. We could get Olivier and Renard to meet us there."

"I sent them to find Kitty." I stayed silent, the only sound being Lisbeth's slowly beating heart, and I saw him glance over at me out of the corner of my eye. The tear streaks down his face were unmistakable. "If I didn't do everything I could to get her back, I couldn't live with myself."

I brushed Lisbeth's hair with the hand holding her head up. She was so still limp. Stop being so limp. Please.

Bump bump.

I took in a ragged breath and pulled her closer to me. "Once I know she's going to be okay, we're going to talk. Man to man."

Arthur nodded. "Understood."

10

A LONG AWAITED CONVERSATION

*W*e drove for as small a time as needed until both of us were certain no humans were nearby. Arthur took the Jeep off-road and found a small clearing for us to put the tent up that I'd brought. He helped me lay Lisbeth down inside it and he examined her again by touching her neck and putting his ear to her breast.

"I need to…" He motioned to her torso and looked up at me for permission. I nodded, so he lifted her shirt to look at her stomach. It was stuck with blood and he almost had to tear it to move it out of the way. If the cuts on her arms were deep, the gashes on her stomach were enormous. I could swear I saw glimpses of things I didn't want to see in those cuts, and I was glad I wasn't squeamish. They hadn't healed. Why hadn't they healed? And that wasn't even the worst bit. There was a large red bruise over half of her side.

Arthur was ready with an explanation. "Internal bleeding. It's why her neck is still broken and the cuts haven't healed, all of her blood is being used to keep her alive." He grabbed his bag and ripped it open so hard the zipper almost broke. Inside he searched for something and pulled it out. He had all the makings of an IV, including a little stand for the blood bag to hang from. "She's unconscious so she can't swallow. If you put blood in her mouth, she'd choke on it." I appreciated how he was answering everything I would've asked if I could actually form words. The graveness of his face was stealing the life from my throat. He handed me the bag to fill and set the IV up, putting the needle into her arm before covering it with tape. "Special vampire needle to pierce the skin." Now he was just talking to keep himself focused.

Slicing my wrist open with one of my teeth, my blood flowed into the bag like a waterfall. Arthur was giving me a hungry look, no doubt he was very thirsty from all the exertion and stress, but he hid it well enough. Once it was full, I handed him the bag and he connected it to the IV line, then he sat down and wiped his forehead, his other hand gripping the tent floor tightly. We both listened to her heartbeat as the blood flowed into her system.

Bump bump. Bump bump.

I took her hand and held it tightly as if it would somehow make her better. I wished with everything I had that it could. I couldn't lose her, not now, not ever.

I needed her forever.

I scrubbed my other hand down my face and tried to

sigh without crying, my thumb flicking her signet wedding ring back and forth. Arthur checked her stomach and I looked down to see some of the bigger cuts start to close. We both let out a breath of relief. He took out a small pillow from his bag and propped her head up, feeling her neck a little to see if it was healing as well.

"You'll have to fill up the bag a few times once it's empty, but I think she'll be okay now."

I wiped at my nose and sniffed. "Thank you. I wouldn't have been able to help her without you."

"Hmm," he said, sitting back down, making the tent floor crinkle. "I doubt that." He took some water from his bag and passed me one before opening his and taking a swig. "I umm... I should check something else." Before I could ask what he meant, he leaned his head in and pressed his ear to her lower stomach.

Oh. My god.

He stayed there for several moments, much longer than seemed necessary. "I thought I heard an echo with her heartbeat. A fetus's heartbeat is very soft at this stage. Humans wouldn't be able to hear it. I can barely make it out, but it's there." His head lifted and he motioned for me to put my ear where he'd laid his.

Bump bump. Bump bump.

I had no words for what I was feeling. Fear that I'd almost lost both my wife and her unborn child. Relief that both had made it through so far. Sadness because it had taken me nineteen years for her to have my child, and it had taken only one try for Arthur to do the same.

Then I forgot all of that, and focused on the tiny heartbeat. Lisbeth had said she would have a girl. A girl with sandy blonde hair and tanned skin, like Arthur.

"Let's have that talk, then," Arthur said when I lifted my head.

"No foreplay, okay." I drank from my water too and went back to clasping Lisbeth's limp hand. "You love my wife." He looked like he was about to say something, but decided not to. "I've gotten used to it over the years because I knew you refused to have anything with her, not after dumping her unceremoniously when I came back."

"It's better for all three of us this way," he assured, watching her still face.

"That's not true." He looked up at me in confusion. "You saw what she was like when you came back ten years ago. She was lost without you. Whether she knows it or not, she loves you as much as she loves me. She fell in love with you when she thought I was dead, and when you ended it, I know something inside her was hurting for you, even as she was in my arms. I know her. I see her. And she loves you." As the words came from my mouth, I realized how much I meant them. Something was changing, and it had nothing to do with the chaos that was going on outside.

He was so focused on her sleeping form, like she was a mirage he had to keep watching or she'd fade away. "She belongs with you."

"I'm not saying she doesn't."

He turned his icy glare to me. "Then what the *hell* are you suggesting, Knight? I'm not going to play games with you, not about her."

"I'm not playing," I told him, running my hands over Lisbeth's ring.

"Then what? You want me to screw her, get her out of my system?" He was as angry as I'd ever seen him, but I wasn't going to back down from this, not anymore. "If I was with her, I'd hurt her again, like I've hurt everyone in my life. I shot my mate in the face for breaking the law, Knight. Did she tell you that? And every night I fall asleep hoping that the day doesn't come where Lisbeth dies because of my mistakes. She's safe with you. You won't hurt her, you won't do anything that causes her harm. I can't promise the same."

So this was what he'd been worried about all this time. *Dumb ass.*

"You're so stupid, Arthur. How about you ask her if she trusts you to keep her safe? I guarantee you she'll say she does." Arthur scoffed, and dared to reach out for Lisbeth's other hand, given our conversation it was very brave of him to do so. "I need you to promise me something. Two things. That's all I'm asking for. For her." I expected resistance or a snide comment, but he just stared at Lisbeth and nodded.

"If it's for her, I'll do anything you ask of me."

Well, here went nothing.

"I want your word that if she ever wants you again, romantically, you'll stop this, 'you belong with Knight' bullshit and be with her. As her lover, as her mate, whatever she wants. I'm still the Alpha mate, so don't go getting funny ideas, but... there. That's it."

Arthur's crystal eyes flicked to me, studying me so hard I almost felt like blushing. "You realize what that will mean, right? I'm not interested in being her friend, or her side piece. If I get any part of her, I want it all. I want everything you get every day. You get to wake up to her every day, you get to see her smile with love in her eyes every time she looks at you. You get to hold her close like you're never letting her go again. You get her ups and downs, you see her in a way no one else does, not even me."

Maybe he did too.

"Sappy, but sure, fine. You get everything I get. No restrictions."

Before I could react, he launched himself across Lisbeth's legs and threw himself into my arms, holding me in our first hug ever, and I felt warm all over weirdly, the way I did when I hugged Lisbeth.

I oddly wanted more hugs from him.

He whispered into my ear, making a tingle spread across my skin. "If you're screwing with me, I'm going to kill you."

"Yeah, yeah," I said, patting his back, and trying to ignore how good it felt being in his embrace. "Remember she calls the shots. If she's not ready for you, you can't say anything. It's been a long time since you two were a thing, she might be too hurt."

"I know, I know." He pulled away and the tear streaks

were back when he returned to his spot at Lisbeth's side. "What was the other thing?" He pretended to have a spec in his eyes so he could wipe at them.

"She literally almost died just now, and I wished that I could've taken her place, that it was me instead, and if our places had been switched, I'm sure I would have died. Things are changing out there so fast, I can't wrap my head around it. The world isn't safe anymore. In keeping with what I just said, I need your word that you'll love my wife if I die, as her mate. That you'll never leave her, not ever."

Arthur didn't respond to what I'd said. We sat next to Lisbeth for a long time, both holding her hands, not speaking, until the sun was slowly fading into the horizon. All the while I could hear her heart beating in her chest, growing stronger with every minute, and the more I focused, the more I could hear the tiny heartbeat coming from her womb.

"I'm cool with it, by the way," I said after the sun had gone down. Arthur looked up at me, startled by my voice after so many hours of silence. "You and her having this baby, I mean. It means a lot to her. I need your word on that too, that if anything happens to this baby, you'll give her another if I'm gone. We both know what it means to her, so get it done. And maybe this time you can go with the traditional method of conception." I pumped my fist at him and he rolled his eyes.

"I can't believe you talk about your own wife like that."

"It's called relationship trust, buddy. I'll always be her number one, even if she chooses you too."

His icy blue eyes still fixed on her face, he held up a fist. "I give you my word."

My eyes widened and my mouth dropped. "Gasp. Our first fist bump." I put my fist up and he lowered his instantly.

"Too slow."

"*I will murder you.*"

Lisbeth slept calmly for several days. I refilled her IV bag as many times as I could, stealing all the snacks Arthur had brought to refuel my blood. Seeing her lying there for so long was making me beside myself with worry, not only for her but also the baby. Arthur calmly explained she'd been hurt so badly that she had slipped into a coma in order for her body to repair itself. I didn't need to be a doctor to know how close she'd been to death. I'd been there once myself, and my beautiful wife was the cause then. This time, I couldn't help feeling that I'd caused her injuries. I should've been by her side the entire time, protecting her from the drones.

Blaming myself wouldn't help, and I knew she'd just tell me I was wrong. I would still carry it with me, a silent reminder of how I'd failed her. Every time she smiled at me, I'd remember that next time I wouldn't fail her again. She'd never be lying there lifeless again, not with me by her side.

I fell asleep every night listening to the sound of two heartbeats. One strong, one infinitesimal. Arthur slept outside, by choice, and drank bagged blood he had in a cooler.

We moved campsites a few times over those lifeless days, getting closer and closer to the remote cabin even though it wasn't a long drive. We weren't willing to move Lisbeth more than we had to. Once we were at the cabin, we'd make a plan. I wouldn't think ahead until Lisbeth was awake again. Arthur kept in touch with everyone on his holo-phone until the signal went dead. We didn't know if that was because of our location, or if cell towers were dropping. Neither of us wanted it to be the latter, and without the holo-phone, we didn't have any way to communicate with anyone because someone forgot to bring a hand radio. Side note: it was Arthur, and it made getting to the cabin a priority, because in addition to a hand radio, we had everything there to survive on our own. Including twinkies.

Day four rolled over, and after a small amount of driving in the front seat with Lisbeth in my lap, we stopped and set up camp again. Arthur helped me lay Lisbeth down on the tent floor, and he put her IV on the stand. He stopped and picked it up to check the lines of measurement on the bag.

"What's up?" I asked, picking up her hand and stroking it with my fingers.

"She's not using much blood now. She can be off the IV. She'll wake up soon I think." He pulled the needle out of her arm and watched the little hole close up instantly. "Healing is automatic. She's doing good." Checking my face first, he laid his head down to check the baby's heartbeat, and then he put the supplies away into his bag. "Baby is fine too."

"You're really good with medicine. Where'd you learn it?"

He didn't look up at me while he fussed in his bag. "I was in charge of the vampire division during the World Wars. There were dozens of us fighting on the front lines for the first war. The second, we tried espionage instead. Less bloodshed. No death. It might surprise you to know that we've always cared about the humans during wartime. I could've served in every war after that instead of the few I chose to be part of, just to ensure the outcome was one we wanted."

"But instead you chose to police your own kind." I kissed Lisbeth's hand again. "Don't think I've forgotten how you chased us like animals."

He glowered at me. "It was my *job*. And I only started doing that because of what happened during World War II. Don't think for one second that that dictator didn't have vampires helping him. I couldn't allow that to happen again."

I whistled low. "Woww. That's... actually interesting. Could you read me that as a bedtime story?" He rolled his eyes, grabbed his bag, and left the tent. I laid down next to my wife, and now that she wasn't hooked up to an IV, I gently pulled her into my arms. Just to be sure, I checked Arthur's position to see if he could hear me before I started talking to her.

"Remember that time when I almost threw up because you were drinking blood?" I chuckled, staring up at the tent ceiling. "I can barely even remember a time when I thought you were repulsive. Just to be clear, I was lying because I thought you were hot, and it wasn't kosher for me to like you. Then I did like you, and I was convinced I'd be like Arthur, loving you from a distance forever. But score, you liked me back." I smelled a rabbit, and then the rabbit's blood. Arthur was hunting for our dinner. "You have to wake up. I almost lost you, and I can't..." I sighed and started petting her long beautiful curls. "I can't go on without you. Not for Jason, not for Kitty, not for Merrick. You're everything." I kissed her forehead and left a wet, salty spot, only to lean my head against it a moment later.

11

TOGETHER

I don't know when I fell asleep, but I woke up to sunlight on the tent top, and I felt someone's fingers stroking my hair. My immediate first thought was Arthur had come in during the night, so I immediately sprang awake and saw Lisbeth staring up at me with a tired smile.

"You're awake. You woke up," I breathed like a prayer. I'd never been so grateful in my entire two hundred and eleven years. Never. She held me tight, and I held her tighter. If I held her tight enough, maybe it would erase the pain and the worry.

"You're squishing me," she whispered, and I let her go enough where she could breathe, but no more. "I was in bad shape, huh?"

I cried and laughed at once. "A bit."

Her lithe fingers flowed through my hair, releasing my built up tension. "Knight." I knotted my hands through her curls. "I'm not dead. I promise I'm not."

"I know, I know." I sniffed and untangled myself from her to wipe my face clean. She wiped her cheeks as well and leaned in to kiss mine before delicately kissing my lips, and I was lost to her, the woman who owned my heart. No kiss could ever convey the depth of my feelings for her. It was like every moment before had been erased, and I needed desperately to show her all over again what she meant to me. Ending our kiss was like cutting off my arm.

"Hey umm, there's something else," I mentioned softly. "Remember that squirt and flirt you did a few weeks ago?"

"Squirt and flirt?" she questioned, eyebrow raised, but then it hit her and she looked down at her stomach. "For real?" Her eyes closed and she focused her senses inward. "I hear the heartbeat. But I was so hurt, how did we both survive?"

"Arthur. And my blood. Mostly my blood. You're welcome, mini-Arthur." I tickled at her belly button and she giggled, trying to get away. Safe from my tickling fingers, she pulled her arms around herself, like she was giving her stomach a hug.

"I get to see her. She'll be in my arms." She smiled contently and looked up at me. "And after her, our daughter will come."

"Score! More Mini-Me's." I crawled over for a kiss on her lush lips. "Happy?" She nodded.

Arthur was outside making noise, and Lisbeth put out a hand for me to help her up. She was still unsteady on her feet so I led her outside holding one hand with the other on her back. Arthur had another rabbit on a spit over a fire covering the forest air with the smell of cooked meat, and he looked up when we came out of the tent. It was his usual blank face, but I saw behind it. He was relieved.

"Hungry?" he asked us, his eyes only on her.

"I love rabbit," she said with a smile. We sat down on either side of her and started enjoying the juicy meat. Arthur gave her extra and I didn't complain. "Remember the first day we met?" she asked me after her first bite. "You had a rabbit cooking, and you wouldn't share it with me." She elbowed me, grinning.

"Near-death Lisbeth is awfully nostalgic," I teased. "Remember the day we first met?" I asked Arthur with a smirk. "I totes kicked your ass."

He gave me an Arthur scowl, but the corners of his mouth were almost teasing. "And then you were naked. I remember."

"Bet you liked what you saw," I chided, shaking a finger at him.

"Wouldn't you like to know." He stood up and started stomping out the fire. "Let's head out. We'll get to the cabin before lunch."

"Wow, you guys took four days to drive like seven hours?" she observed, licking her fingers. I kissed her and tasted meat with her normal flavor. Yummy.

"No judging, only kisses," I ordered, and got as many kisses as I could in the back seat of the jeep until we arrived at our private drive. I punched in the security code at the fence and it retracted back for us to drive through. Fancy, I know. The unpaved drive wound past forests of pine trees and beech trees, dogwoods and red oak. The road went up and twisted around until we were in front of a large lake and our lovely cabin.

I'd gotten *so* lucky all over this place.

Arthur was appraising it with a look I could call impressed. "This is nice. I like it."

Wait 'til you hear how much booty happened here.

"We'll get the radio running and send a message out. Everything runs on a generator, so we'll still have power." Lisbeth hopped out of the jeep and picked up her backpack. I was right behind her with my bag and waited for her to unlock the door before immediately tossing myself onto one of the couches in the living room.

Arthur came in behind her, wrinkling his nose. "Do you two clean this place? I can smell... things."

"I'll pretend you never said that," Lisbeth deflected, and disappeared into one of the bedrooms.

"Remember that time you agreed to never talk about her love life? Good times."

He dropped his bag and sniffed at a chair before sitting on it. Nope, that one wasn't safe, but I kept silent. It was probably a good thing he didn't have a black light. At least I hoped he didn't. "You weren't there."

"I was outside the door, bro. You'd be surprised at the things I overheard in that castle."

"Oh, so you heard that time when I asked her if my butt looked nice?" The corners of his mouth turned up ever so slightly.

"I know you're joking, but bruh. Not cool."

"Remember that time you almost died wearing a man bun?" Lisbeth shouted from the bedroom. "Classic." Arthur covered his hand with his mouth, but I could still hear him laughing. I threw a pillow at him, he dodged it, and it sailed to slam into Lisbeth's face when she came out of the bedroom because she wasn't paying attention. Unfazed, she walked over to us and glanced at where Arthur was sitting. "And for your information, we did it in that chair." He immediately jumped up and she held out her hand to me for a high five.

"Love you, babe," I told her, slapping her hand.

She did a double finger gun snap at Arthur. "That's for teasing my husband." Pulling it from her pocket, she handed Arthur the radio. "Here, I don't know how to use it. We need to find Kitty and Jason." He took it and walked over to the kitchen to start fiddling with the dials to find the right frequency. Lisbeth sat next to my legs, slowly moving to lean over me. "Well, I haven't showered in four days. How about you?" Her mouth curved up in that way I liked.

"Arthur get out."

Feeling fresh and clean after our shower, we went to the kitchen to start making dinner. I saw Arthur standing next to the lake, looking out over the beautiful blue water. Lisbeth put her arms around me from behind and peeked her head out to see what I was looking at. Her wet curls brushed against my arm and we watched the stoic warrior against the water.

"He was worried too. I'm not the only one who almost lost you," I said, kissing her hand. "He cried."

She looked at me in disbelief. "You're lying."

"I'm not." I lifted her hand and kissed her knuckles. "Go tell your boyfriend that we're making dinner and he'd better help out or he doesn't get any."

She lifted up on her tiptoes to kiss my cheek, and then she walked barefoot outside to where Arthur stood. I craned to hear them, but they didn't say anything until they both turned and walked back inside the house.

"I managed to contact Olivier," he said, putting the radio on the counter. We waited for him to say more, hoping he had news about Kitty. "The epidemic is overtaking the planet. They're trying to save as many as possible, but there's almost no point. Alistair has destroyed everything." He sat down on one of the bar stools and clasped his hands in front of him. "I should've..." He let out a ragged breath and Lisbeth came to grip his hand in hers. She reached back to me with her other hand and I took it.

"I swear to god if you cry, I will lose it," Lisbeth scolded. "We're not going to sit in this cabin and whine about what we should've done. We're going out there to find our children. I don't care where they are or how long it takes. If the world is being re-written, I want my children by my side. And both of you."

"*Our?*" Arthur questioned, his eyes still cast down to hide any moisture on them.

"We're having a child together. You're family. Get used to it." She let go of his hand, wiped at her nose, and squeezed his shoulder. "Let's make dinner. We're leaving tomorrow morning."

We ate spaghetti and drank wine. It was almost normal. Me cracking jokes, Lisbeth laughing, and Arthur telling us to grow up as he struggled not to crack a smile when he looked at Lisbeth's face. You'd have never known the world was going to hell outside. We went to bed and woke up the next morning, packed our bags, and stood on the front porch planning where we'd go.

"I think we should leave the jeep, just walk off-road," Lisbeth suggested, running her hands down her backpack straps. "The drones will be in the cities with the gas stations. It's not worth the risk."

Arthur was marking a path on the map and nodded. "Agreed. We have tents, rations. We'll have to restock but we can do it safely. There's only one problem."

"Blood supply," Lisbeth noted quietly. I saw Arthur making notes on where he could raid some hospitals.

"Damn it," I complained with a sigh. "Arthur can drink from me. If I get a stiffy from it, that's on you."

Lisbeth put her hand on my arm. "No, no one is asking you to do that. Especially since I'm expecting and I'll need more blood from you."

"I don't care. We have to. If he continues drinking bagged blood, he'll get weaker, and we need him strong. Arthur, we cool?" He nodded, way too cool with this arrangement. *Pervert.* "Cool. Anything else?"

Lisbeth shrugged. "I think we've got it from here."

"You're lucky your cabin had all the supplies we needed," Arthur said, slinging his bag over his shoulder.

"Fist bump?" she asked him with a smile.

"Never."

"You're literally the worst." She tossed her long curls and I saw for the briefest moment Arthur smiling at her where she couldn't see.

"You two are the cutest," I cooed playfully.

"Oh my god, can we just go?" She stomped forward off the porch and we followed after her, into a world that was changing with every moment, but we'd both be there to keep her safe.

Together.

NOTES

1. THE CARNIVAL OF HORRORS

1. Con queso: With cheese.

2. MUSINGS IN PIG LATIN

1. Iway ikelay ouryay uttbay: I like your butt.
2. Opstay aringstay atway ymay aughter'sday uttbay: Stop staring at my daughter's butt.
3. Ancay eway opstay alkingtay aboutway om'smay uttbay: Can we stop talking about Mom's butt?

Glossary

*B*icus: A collective term for the sibling creatures known as Incubus and Succubus.

Bonding ceremony: A vampire wedding involving a vow between the couple, exchanging of each other's blood, and mixing their blood together through a cut on their wrists.

Born vampires: The product of an Incubus and human female union. They can turn humans, create drones, and give birth to new vampires. Born vampires must drink fresh human blood every day. Drinking bagged human blood cannot sustain them and will cause them to slowly starve.

Companion: A term for the humans that serve vampires. They sign a ten year contract and are chosen by a vampire to live in their rooms, and be willingly bitten once a day to feed the vampire. Once their contract is up they can either renew it, or they can leave with a promised sum of money upon contract termination.

Council: A group comprised of the heads of each vampire Order. They oversee all vampires, pass judgement for infractions, and direct the vampire Hunters.

Dhampir: The product of a vampire and human union. None were known to exist as the two species typically do not mix romantically.

Frenzy: A state vampires reach when they are so starved of blood their body can no longer cope. They become wild, their eyes glow red, and they will attack until their hunger is sated.

Hunters: A group comprised solely of Born vampires whose sole purpose is to hunt down any vampire that has broken the law, and either bring them to justice or execute them.

Incubus: A creature of seduction, built for the sole purpose of coupling with female humans to create new Born vampires. If an Incubus falls in love, they develop a distinctive scent.

Lycans: The product of a Primal werewolf and human female union. They can shift into a wolf whenever they like.

Primal werewolves: Originally human men who have been scratched by a succubus, turning them to a werewolf when the full moon rises.

The Bicus plane: A mystical realm only accessible to those with the blood of the Bicus. Time moves differently inside the plane, moving slower or faster than Earth depending on the moment.

The Order Acilino: Location in Spain, name translates to "Eagle."

The Order Bête: Location in Canada, name translates to "Beast."

The Order Dedliwan: Location in Australia, name translates to "Deadly."

The Order Engel: Location in Greenland, name translates to "Angel."

The Order Gennadi: Location in Russia, name translates to "Noble."

The Order Janiccat: Location in Malaysia, name translates to "Born."

The Order Khalid: Location in Algeria, name translates to "Immortal."

The Order Oleander: Location in the United States, name translates to "Poisonous."

The Order Qiángdù: Location in China, name translates to "Strength."

The Order Raposa: Location in Brazil, name translates to "Fox."

The Order Safed: Location in India, name translates to "Undamaged."

The Order Sangre: Location in Mexico, name translates to "Blood."

The turned vampires: Vampires that used to be humans and have been. Note: the word "turned" in reference to this type of vampire is never capitalized, hence referring to them as "the turned" to avoid this. They cannot turn humans, or give birth. The turned must drink human blood every day. Unlike the Born vampires, the turned vampires can survive on bagged blood.

Vaewolf: The product of a Primal werewolf or Lycan and a vampire union. They can shift into a wolf whenever they like, they have vampire fangs, and they require blood to heal if they are seriously injured. They do not require daily blood like vampires do.

Vipyre: The product of an Incubus and vampire female union. An incredibly rare creature, only one has ever been known to exist, but it is most likely due to lost knowledge as these creatures have been written about in Incubi lore.

Bathory Family

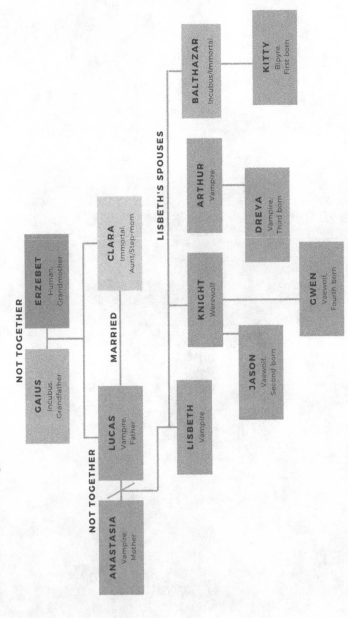

NOT TOGETHER

| GAIUS | ERZEBET |
| Incubus, Grandfather | Human, Grandmother |

MARRIED

CLARA
Immortal, Aunt/Step-mom

NOT TOGETHER

| ANASTASIA | LUCAS |
| Vampire, Mother | Vampire, Father |

LISBETH
Vampire

LISBETH'S SPOUSES

| KNIGHT | ARTHUR | BALTHAZAR |
| Werewolf | Vampire | Incubus/Immortal |

JASON
Vaewolf, Second born

GWEN
Vaewolf, Fourth born

DREYA
Vampire, Third born

KITTY
Bipyre, First born

Castle of the Order Oleander

Road to town

Front gate

Underground garage ramp

Social Area

Picnic Tables

Life-sized Chessboard

Back gate

Christiaung River

ABOUT THE AUTHOR

Photo by Elizabeth Dunlap

Elizabeth Dunlap is the author of several fantasy books, including the Born Vampire series. She's never wanted to be anything else in her life, except maybe a vampire. She lives in Texas with her boyfriend, their daughter, and a very sleepy chihuahua named Deyna.

You can find her online at
www.elizabethdunlap.com

CPSIA information can be obtained
at www.ICGtesting.com
Printed in the USA
LVHW041533231120
672481LV00003B/749